1

AN EARLY START

Morning light crawled through the grimy window like a hesitant visitor, casting slanted beams across the cramped tenement room and illuminating dust motes that pirouetted in its glow. Mercy Whitfield's eyes fluttered open at the familiar cacophony of Seven Dials stirring to life—vendors' shouts already echoing between buildings, children's laughter rising from the alley below, and the persistent clatter of cart wheels on cobblestones.

She stretched her nine-year-old limbs beneath the threadbare blanket, her nightgown twisting around her ankles. The fabric, once white, had yellowed with age and countless washings, yet it remained soft against her skin—a testament to her mother's meticulous care even of the simplest things.

Across the room, Sarah Whitfield sat perched at their rickety wooden table, her slender fingers dancing across a pile of fabric scraps. Morning sun caught in her dark brown hair, highlighting strands of premature silver at her temples. Despite the early hour, she was already deep in concentration, her needle flashing in and out of silk like a silver fish darting through water.

"You're awake, my little sparrow." Her mother's voice filled their small quarters with warmth that belied the perpetual damp of the walls. "Did you sleep well?"

Mercy nodded, padding across the uneven floorboards. "I dreamt of flowers, Mama. Great big ones in colours I've never seen."

"That's the Lord sending you beauty." Her mother's blue eyes crinkled at the corners as she smiled, her face momentarily transformed from weary to radiant. "Come, I've something to show you."

The table before her mother was littered with an artist's palette of threads—crimson, indigo, gold, and forest green—alongside fabric scraps salvaged from the fine houses where she found work. Her hands, though roughened by labour, moved with the precision of a master craftsman as she beckoned Mercy closer.

"Today, we shall create something beautiful together." Her mother drew Mercy to her side, guiding the child's small fingers over a square of cream-coloured linen. "Lady Harrington's daughter is to be married, and they've commissioned a handkerchief with roses and forget-me-nots."

Mercy's eyes widened. "Will they pay extra for that?"

"Indeed they will." Her mother nodded, tucking a loose strand behind Mercy's ear. "Enough perhaps for meat this Sunday, and maybe—" She paused, her expression softening. "Maybe a bit of ribbon for your hair."

Mercy's fingers brushed against a sampler pinned to the table's edge—her own work from yesterday, the stitches uneven but improving. She traced the pattern with reverent fingertips, pride swelling in her chest.

"Your hands were made for this work, Mercy." Sarah

guided her daughter's fingers through the motions of a French knot. "Such fine, nimble fingers. God gives each of us gifts, and He's blessed you with special talents."

Something flickered in Mercy's memory then—strong arms lifting her high, a deep laugh rumbling against her ear, the scratch of a woollen uniform against her cheek. The shadow of her father passed through her mind, gone before she could grasp it fully.

Her gaze drifted to the small wooden box on the mantelpiece, where her father's medals rested alongside his folded cap. Though she had few memories of him—just fragments of warmth and safety—his presence remained in their tiny home through these treasured objects and her mother's stories.

Her mother followed her gaze. "Thinking of your father this morning?"

Mercy nodded, her throat suddenly tight. "I wish I remembered him better."

Her mother set down her needle and turned in her chair, drawing Mercy between her knees. Her hands, smelling of soap and cotton, framed her daughter's face.

"Your father was a soldier, every bit a protector for us." Her voice softened, carrying both pride and sorrow. "He stood tall in that uniform, you know. When he walked through Seven Dials, people would step aside—not from fear, but respect."

She glanced at the military pension notice tucked beside their Bible. "He made certain we would have something, even after he was gone. Not much, perhaps, but it shows his forethought, his love."

"Did he know how to sew like us?" Mercy asked, leaning into her mother's embrace.

Her mother laughed, the sound brightening their humble room. "Actually, he did! He mended his own uniform when needed. Said a soldier who couldn't repair his own gear wasn't much of a soldier at all." She squeezed Mercy's shoulders. "He would have been so proud of your nimble fingers, little one."

Mercy's eyes shone as she imagined her father, sitting at this very table, teaching her mother the neat, practical stitches a soldier might need. The image filled a space inside her that often felt hollow.

"Now then," Her mother said, returning to the present moment, "shall we begin? Lady Harrington expects perfection, and perfection requires an early start."

2

SO MUCH MORE

A sudden commotion erupted outside their window, startling Mercy's needle to a halt mid-stitch. Two vendors' voices rose above the morning bustle of Seven Dials, their argument about bread prices growing heated with each exchange.

"Five pence? You're a dirty thief, Morris!"

"It's quality flour! Go elsewhere if you don't like it!"

Mercy rose from her seat and peered through the grimy window. Her bright green eyes caught the scene below—two red-faced men gesturing wildly as a small crowd gathered to watch. Behind them, a ragged child slipped an apple from an unattended cart, disappearing into an alley before anyone noticed.

"That's enough of that," her mother said, gently pulling Mercy back to their work. "The world outside has its troubles, but in here, we make something beautiful."

The smells of Seven Dials wafted through their cracked window—fresh bread from the bakery three doors down mingled with the less pleasant odours of chamber pots emptied into gutters and unwashed bodies pressed too close together in crowded tenements.

"Do you think Lady Harrington's house smells of roses all the time?" Mercy asked, settling back at the table.

Her mother laughed softly. "Perhaps, though I imagine even grand houses have their unpleasant corners. Now, watch carefully."

Her mother's needle danced across the fabric, creating tiny, perfect stitches that seemed to bloom beneath her fingertips. Mercy leaned forward, entranced by the motion.

"See how the needle glides beneath the fabric?" Her mother demonstrated a particularly delicate rosebud. "Each stitch is a prayer, Mercy. A prayer of thanks for the gift of our hands, for the thread that feeds us."

Mercy nodded solemnly. She picked up her own needle, attempting to mimic her mother's graceful movements. Her first few stitches puckered the fabric, but by the fourth try, something changed. The needle seemed to find its own path, guided by some instinct in her small fingers.

"Look, Mama!" she exclaimed, holding up a nearly perfect section of stem stitch.

Her mother's face brightened with pride. "What did I tell you? Nimble fingers blessed by God Himself." She kissed the top of Mercy's head. "You'll surpass me one day, little sparrow."

As the morning stretched into afternoon, they worked side by side, the steady rhythm of their needles punctuated by her mother's soft voice reciting Scripture. The words flowed like a gentle stream, offering comfort against the harsh realities that waited beyond their door.

"'Consider the lilies of the field,'" Her mother recited, her needle never faltering, "'how they grow; they toil not, neither do they spin. And yet I say unto you that even Solomon in all his glory was not arrayed like one of these.'"

"What does that mean, Mama?" Mercy asked, tongue caught between her teeth as she concentrated on a particularly challenging section.

"It means that God provides, even when we cannot see how." Her mother paused, setting down her work. "Shall we pray together?"

Mercy nodded, placing her needle carefully on the table and folding her hands as her mother had taught her. Sarah's work-worn hands enveloped her daughter's smaller ones, and both closed their eyes.

"Heavenly Father," Her mother began, her voice steady and sure, "we thank You for the gift of this day, for the work of our hands, and for Your provision. Help us to trust in Your plan, even when the path seems uncertain. Bless this work that it might please those who commissioned it, and that it might continue to feed and shelter us. In Your holy name, amen."

"Amen," Mercy echoed, feeling the warmth of her mother's faith wrap around her like a blanket.

The light shifted as the day progressed, casting golden beams across their small table. The handkerchief took shape beneath their combined efforts—roses and forget-me-nots intertwined in an elegant dance around the edges, with space in the centre for the bride's monogram.

"Hold it up to the light," Her mother instructed, her eyes crinkling with pleasure.

Mercy did as she was told, her heart swelling with pride as the afternoon sun illuminated their work. The stitches were even, the design harmonious. It was more than mere sewing; it was art born of necessity, beauty created amidst want.

"It's the most beautiful thing I've ever seen," Mercy breathed.

"And much of it by your hand," Her mother replied, pulling her daughter close. "You have a gift, Mercy. A true gift."

As dusk approached, the sounds of Seven Dials changed— pub doors swung open, work-weary men and women trudged home, children were called in from their play. But in their small room above the cobbler's shop, Mercy and her mother remained in their own world of creation.

Mercy watched her mother's face in the fading light—the fine lines around her eyes, the slight hollow of her cheeks, the serene set of her mouth despite the persistent cough that had troubled her through winter. She saw strength there, a quiet determination that had kept them fed and sheltered after her father's death.

"Mama," she said suddenly, "when I grow up, I want to be just like you."

Her mother smiled, though her eyes glistened suspiciously. "Oh, my darling girl. I believe you'll be so much more."

3
ENOUGH

Mercy's stomach growled as she sat beside her mother at their small table. Two days had passed since they'd delivered the bride's handkerchief to Lady Harrington's residence. The butler had accepted it with a curt nod, promising payment would follow. True to his word, a footman had appeared that very morning with an envelope.

Now her mother emptied the contents onto the scarred wooden surface—five shillings and threepence. Her fingers, red and slightly swollen from yesterday's washing, carefully arranged the coins in neat stacks.

"Is it enough, Mama?" Mercy asked, watching her mother's face.

Her mother eyes grew distant, fixed on some point beyond their cramped room. The lines around her mouth deepened. For a moment, Mercy glimpsed something raw in her mother's expression—fear, perhaps, or worry too heavy to share.

"It will do," Her mother said finally. "The rent's due tomorrow—that's four shillings. We've bread enough for three days, and I've that mending for Mrs Finch to finish."

Mercy nodded, understanding the arithmetic of survival even at nine. One shilling and threepence remained for everything else—coal, candles, thread, food beyond bread.

"But what about the meat? And my ribbon?" The words slipped out before Mercy could stop them.

Her mother's hand paused mid-count. She turned to Mercy, her smile returning though it didn't quite reach her eyes.

"The ribbon must wait, little sparrow." She touched Mercy's cheek. "These coins may not build us a palace, but my love for you, dear Mercy, will always create our home."

Mercy leaned into her mother's touch, ashamed of her disappointment. "I shouldn't have asked. I don't need a ribbon."

"Wanting pretty things isn't wrong," Her mother said, pulling Mercy close. "God made beauty too, not just necessity. We'll have your ribbon someday."

As twilight settled over Seven Dials, they arranged their current projects on the table—a tablecloth for the vicar's wife, handkerchiefs for a gentleman on Savile Row, and mending for three different households. Sarah lit a single candle, its glow illuminating their work.

"See how lovely they look together?" Her mother whispered. "Like a garden we're planting, stitch by stitch."

Mercy nodded, watching the candlelight dance across the fabrics. They sat close, shoulders touching, the day's disappointments softening in the gentle light.

"Tomorrow I'll take you with me to deliver Mrs Finch's mending," Her mother said. "She mentioned her daughter needs a christening gown embroidered. Perhaps they'll consider us."

Mercy smiled, feeling the familiar flutter of possibility.

Tomorrow held no guarantees, but tonight they had enough— enough light to see by, enough work for their hands, enough love to sustain them.

4
WINTER'S CHILL

Mercy traced her fingers over the frost-laced windowpane, drawing patterns that disappeared beneath her touch. Outside, Seven Dials lay beneath a blanket of grimy snow, the usual bustle of street vendors muted by winter's harsh embrace. The breath of those few brave souls who ventured outside hung in cloudy puffs before their pinched faces. From her vantage point on the third floor, Mercy watched a mother tug her protesting child through the slush, their shoulders hunched against the cold.

Six years had passed since that day with the coins on the table. Six years of lessons at her mother's side, of prayers whispered by candlelight, of stitches growing finer with each passing season. And now this—her fifteenth winter, marked by a chill that seemed to have settled not just in the air but deep within her bones.

She pressed her forehead against the cold glass and closed her eyes. The memory came unbidden, sharp and clear as yesterday.

"Mercy, come away from the window, you'll catch your

death." Her mother's voice had been thin, like thread pulled too tight, ready to snap.

Mercy had turned to find her mother huddled by their meagre hearth, wrapped in the faded blue shawl that had once belonged to Mercy's grandmother. Between her fingers, she held a tiny scrap of fabric—a doll's dress the colour of spring violets.

"Is that for me, Mama?" Mercy had asked, knowing it was her birthday, though they rarely had means to celebrate properly.

Her mother's fingers trembled as she tried to thread her needle, the firelight catching the silver strands that had appeared in her dark hair seemingly overnight. Her cheeks, once full and pink, had hollowed, and the skin stretched taut across her cheekbones. Still, Sarah summoned a smile that lit her tired blue eyes.

"Fifteen years ago today, God blessed me with the greatest gift." The needle slipped from her fingers, and frustration flickered across her face. "These old hands aren't what they used to be."

Mercy had knelt beside her mother, retrieving the needle and threading it with practiced ease. "Let me help."

Her mother's cool hand had cupped her cheek. "Look at you, teaching the teacher now."

Together they had stitched the tiny garment, her mother directing when her cough allowed, Mercy executing the delicate work. As darkness fell, the doll's dress lay complete between them, a small victory against the encroaching shadows.

"For your collection," she had whispered, pressing it into Mercy's palm. "Every girl should have something pretty on her birthday."

The memory faded, leaving Mercy staring at her reflection

in the frosted glass. She barely recognised the solemn-faced young woman who stared back.

Three weeks after her birthday, the cough that had plagued her mother for months grew violent. It came in savage bursts that left her gasping, her handkerchief spotted with blood she tried to hide.

"It's nothing," she insisted when Mercy expressed concern. "Just the damp air."

But one grey morning, Mercy woke to find her mother unable to rise from bed, her breath rattling in her chest like dried leaves in winter wind.

"Fetch Mrs Abernathy," her mother whispered, her voice barely audible. "Tell her I need a posset for this chill."

Mercy had run barefoot down the narrow stairs to their neighbour, returning with the kind-hearted widow who took one look at Sarah and crossed herself.

"Child," Mrs Abernathy had murmured, "your mother needs more than a posset."

The next three days blurred together in Mercy's mind — Mrs Abernathy's herbal remedies, the parish doctor's brief visit and grim pronouncement, nights spent holding her mother's hand as fever burned through her frail body.

On the third night, as rain lashed against their window, her mother's eyes had opened with surprising clarity.

"Mercy," she called, her voice stronger than it had been in days.

Mercy had crawled onto the bed beside her, careful not to jostle her mother's pain-wracked body. "I'm here, Mama."

Her mother's fingers, once so nimble with needle and thread, clutched weakly at Mercy's sleeve. "My sewing box— it's yours now. Everything I know, I've taught you."

"Don't talk like that," Mercy had pleaded, tears streaming

down her face. "You'll be better by spring. We'll take that commission for the christening gown."

Her mother's smile was gentle but knowing. "Listen to me, child. The world can be cruel, but you have a gift. Your hands can create beauty from nothing." A coughing fit seized her, and Mercy held her until it passed, leaving Sarah even weaker than before.

"The Bible," Her mother whispered when she could speak again. "Read to me."

Mercy had reached for the small, worn Bible that had been her mother's constant companion. With trembling fingers, she turned to the Psalms, her mother's favourite.

"The Lord is my shepherd; I shall not want," Mercy read, her voice breaking on the familiar words.

Her mother's eyes had closed, her breathing growing more laboured. When Mercy paused, uncertain if her mother still listened, her eyelids fluttered open.

"God has a plan," she whispered, her voice fading with each word. "Even when we can't see it, even when the path is dark. Remember that, my Mercy."

"I will, Mama," Mercy had promised, clutching her mother's cold hand between her own.

"My good girl," Her mother breathed. "My gift from God."

Those were the last words Sarah Whitfield spoke. Before dawn broke, she slipped away, leaving Mercy alone in the world.

THE FUNERAL HAD BEEN BRIEF, a pauper's burial in the churchyard of St Dunstan's. The cobbler, Mr Thompson, who worked in the shop beneath Mercy's home, had bought a simple wooden marker, a kindness Mercy hadn't expected. A handful of neighbours had gathered—Mrs Abernathy, the baker who some-times gave them day-old bread, two women who had commissioned embroidery from Sarah over the years.

Mercy stood alone beside the freshly-turned earth, the small Bible clutched to her chest. The winter wind cut through her thin black dress, a hastily dyed work frock that was her only concession to mourning attire. No tears came; they had been spent during those long nights of vigil.

As the others drifted away, murmuring awkward condo-lences, Mercy remained. The finality of it struck her then—the mound of dirt that covered her mother, the silence where her gentle voice had been, the empty room that awaited her return.

"What do I do now, Mama?" she whispered to the cold air.

No answer came save the rattling of bare branches over-head and the distant sounds of Seven Dials carrying on, indif-ferent to her loss.

5
FOUR DAYS

Three days after the funeral, Mercy clutched her mother's sewing box to her chest, its familiar weight offering little comfort as she climbed the narrow staircase to Mr Edwards' rooms above the adjacent building. Each step felt heavier than the last. The back rent loomed large in her mind —four weeks now, with no means to pay it.

She knocked timidly, her knuckles barely making a sound against the weathered door.

"Who's there?" A gruff voice barked from within.

"It's Mercy Whitfield, sir. From the room above Thompson's shop."

The door swung open to reveal her landlord's imposing figure. Mr Edwards stood there in his shirtsleeves, suspenders hanging loose at his sides, his broad face flushed from drink despite the early hour.

"The seamstress's girl." His bloodshot eyes narrowed. "Come about the rent, have you? About time."

Mercy swallowed hard. "That's why I've come, sir. My mother—she passed three days ago."

"Aye, heard about that. Shame." He crossed his arms, leaning against the doorframe. "Don't change what's owed, though, does it?"

"I haven't got it all just yet, sir." The words tumbled out in a rush. "But I can work. I can sew nearly as fine as Mother did. If you'd allow me a fortnight to—"

"A fortnight?" Mr Edwards snorted. "Four weeks behind already, and you want another two? What do you take me for, girl? A charity?"

"No, sir, I—"

"I've got three families waiting for that room. Willing to pay up front, they are." He straightened, towering over her. "You'll be out by week's end if I don't see the full amount. That's being generous, considering."

The finality in his tone hit Mercy like a physical blow. "Please, sir. I've nowhere else—"

"Not my concern, is it?" He made to close the door. "Four days. Then I'll have the constable clear whatever's left."

The door slammed shut, leaving Mercy trembling on the landing. The wooden stairs seemed to sway beneath her feet as she descended, clutching the banister for support.

Four days. The words echoed in her mind, a death knell for the only home she had ever known.

6

IMPOSSIBLE

Mercy returned to their—no, her—small room above the cobbler's shop. The space felt cavernous without her mother's gentle presence. Four days to pay a month's rent seemed an impossible task, yet Sarah Whitfield had raised a daughter who wouldn't surrender to despair.

"God has a plan," she whispered to herself, her mother's favourite phrase now a lifeline to which she desperately clung.

She set her mother's sewing box on the table and lifted the worn mahogany lid. The familiar creak of its hinges brought tears to her eyes. Inside lay Sarah's legacy—dozens of cotton and silk threads wound on small wooden spools, arranged by colour; packets of needles sorted by size; thimbles polished from years of use; and scraps of fine fabrics salvaged from previous commissions. Each item had its place, just as her mother had taught her.

"Each stitch is a prayer," Mercy murmured, running her fingers over a spool of crimson silk.

Her mother's last commission — a set of handkerchiefs for

Mrs Combs — remained unfinished. Mercy took up the delicate linen and examined the half-completed monogram. Three hours later, she completed the set with stitches so fine they rivalled her mother's own work.

The next morning, heart pounding, Mercy presented herself at Mrs Combs' townhouse, only to be met by a suspicious housekeeper at the servants' entrance.

"The elder Mrs Whitfield always handled these matters," the woman said, eyeing the small package in Mercy's hands.

"My mother has passed, ma'am. I've completed the commission myself."

The housekeeper's expression softened momentarily before hardening again. "Wait here."

Mercy stood in the cold for nearly half an hour before the housekeeper returned.

"Mistress says the work is acceptable, but not quite up to her expectations." She handed Mercy a few coins—half the promised amount. "She won't be requiring your services again."

Mercy fought back tears as she pocketed the meagre payment. The coins felt heavy against her leg as she made her way back through the busy streets of London.

Mr Thompson, the kindly cobbler who had arranged her mother's marker, allowed Mercy to set up in the corner of his shop the following day. She displayed her needlework and offered mending services to his customers. A few local women brought torn shirts and frayed hems, but paid only pennies for work that took hours.

"They've their own troubles, lass," Mr Thompson said as he hammered a sole onto a boot. "Times are hard for everyone."

By the third day, Mercy's fingers were raw from constant sewing, yet her saved coins wouldn't cover even half the rent owed. Desperation drove her to seek out other seamstresses in Seven Dials, hoping for advice or perhaps shared work.

Mrs Finch, another local seamstress Mercy knew, answered her door with a crying infant on her hip and three small children clinging to her skirts.

"I'm sorry for your loss, truly I am," she said, bouncing the fussing baby. "But I've barely enough work to feed my own. The fine houses don't want to see me on their doorsteps with these little ones in tow, and my husband's been without work these three months."

Mercy visited five more seamstresses that afternoon. Each door revealed a similar story—women struggling to survive, unable to spare work or advice for an orphaned girl.

Mrs Winslow, a stern-faced woman known for her embroidery, gave the harshest response. "The wealthy ladies want experienced hands working on their finery, not some child who's barely grown. Find yourself a position in service, girl. That's the best you can hope for now."

As twilight fell on the third day, Mercy counted her earnings at the small table where she and her mother had spent countless hours sewing together. The total fell woefully short. Tomorrow Mr. Edwards would expect his payment, and she had failed.

She opened her mother's Bible, seeking comfort in the familiar words. A verse from Psalms caught her eye: "When my father and my mother forsake me, then the Lord will take me up."

Mercy closed the book and glanced around the room that had been her entire world. Everything that wouldn't fit in her mother's sewing box would have to be left behind. The thought of abandoning her home sent a fresh wave of grief through her, but she had no choice.

Tomorrow she would have to face Mr Edwards with insufficient funds and nowhere to go. The streets of Seven Dials would become her home, and she would join the ranks of London's forgotten poor.

7
STREETS OF THORNS

Morning arrived with harsh, grey light filtering through the small window. Mercy had not slept. Her few belongings sat packed beside the door—a bundle of clothes tied with string, her mother's Bible wrapped carefully in a scrap of cloth, and the precious sewing box that held her only means of survival.

A heavy knock rattled the door precisely at nine o'clock.

"Time's up, girl," Mr Edwards called, his voice carrying through the thin wood.

Mercy's fingers trembled as she smoothed her threadbare dress. Mother had always insisted they present themselves with dignity, no matter their circumstances. She took a final glance around the barren room—the table where she'd learned to sew, the small hearth where they'd shared countless meals, the corner where her mother had drawn her final breath.

"Coming, sir," she answered, her voice steadier than she felt.

Mr Edwards stood in the narrow hallway, arms crossed over his substantial belly. Behind him loitered two rough-looking men, clearly brought to enforce the eviction if necessary.

"I've the money I could gather, sir," Mercy said, holding out a pitiful collection of coins. "Perhaps I could pay the remainder next—"

"Not enough," Edwards cut her off without even glancing at her outstretched hand. "Told you four days. Been more than generous, considering."

One of the men shifted impatiently. "We haven't got all day, Edwards."

"Right then. Out you go, girl. New tenants moving in this afternoon."

Mercy clutched her mother's sewing box against her chest. "Please, sir. My mother always paid on time before she fell ill. Surely—"

"Your mother ain't here, is she?" Edwards's face softened fractionally. "Look, I'm not heartless. Take your things and go. No need for the constable to get involved."

The larger of the two men stepped forward, reaching for her arm. Mercy flinched away.

"I can walk out myself, thank you," she said, summoning every ounce of dignity her mother had instilled in her.

She gathered her bundle and Bible, balanced the sewing box carefully atop them, and stepped into the hallway. The stairwell that had once felt like home now seemed like a descent into the unknown. Each step carried her further from safety, from the memories of her mother's voice, from everything familiar.

"Remember who you are, my love," her mother's voice whispered in her mind. *"A child of God, not of circumstance."*

At the bottom of the stairs, Mr Thompson stood in the doorway of his cobbler's shop, his weathered face creased with concern.

"Mercy, lass. I wish I could offer you a place, but the missus and I barely have room for our own."

"You've been kind enough, Mr Thompson," Mercy replied, forcing a smile. "Thank you for everything."

She stepped out onto the street, the morning bustle of Seven Dials swirling around her. Vendors called their wares, carriages rattled past, people hurried by with barely a glance at the girl carrying her world in her arms. No one noticed one more person without a home.

For hours, Mercy wandered the streets she'd known all her life, suddenly seeing them through different eyes. Alleyways that had seemed merely shortcuts now looked like potential shelters. Shopkeepers who had nodded politely at her and her mother now regarded her with suspicion as she lingered too long in their doorways.

She tried the parish church first, hoping for sanctuary, but found the doors locked between services. At the workhouse gates, she heard the wailing from within and remembered her mother's warnings: "Better the streets than that place, Mercy. They separate families there. They break the spirit."

As the afternoon wore on, hunger gnawed at her stomach. She had not eaten since the previous night, saving her few remaining pennies. The weight of her belongings grew heavier with each passing hour.

Dusk fell early in the February chill, bringing with it a fine, penetrating drizzle. The lamps along the main streets flickered to life, but the side streets remained in shadows. Mercy found herself in a narrow passage off Neal Street, sheltered somewhat by an overhanging upper story. She sank down into a doorway, arranging her skirts to keep them from the wet cobblestones.

The sewing box sat on her lap, her fingers tracing its familiar contours in the gathering darkness. The streets grew quieter as shopkeepers closed their businesses and respectable folk retreated to their homes. Only the desperate, the drunken, and the dangerous remained abroad.

Mercy's heart pounded against her ribs as unfamiliar footsteps approached and then passed her hiding place. The shadows seemed to grow larger around her, looming threats in every corner. Cold seeped through her thin clothes and into her bones until she shivered uncontrollably.

"Please, Lord," she whispered, pressing her forehead against the rough wood of her mother's sewing box. "I don't know what to do now."

8

THE STREETS OF SEVEN DIALS

Another cold morning dawned, the third since Mercy's eviction. She unfolded her stiff limbs from the cramped doorway where she'd spent the night, wincing as circulation returned. Her stomach growled—a familiar companion these past days. The half-slice of bread she'd saved from yesterday would have to suffice until she found work or charity.

Mercy gathered her few possessions, carefully tucking her mother's Bible inside her shawl to protect it from the damp. The precious sewing box remained clutched against her chest as she ventured into the awakening streets.

Seven Dials transformed with daylight. Shopkeepers unlocked doors, housemaids beat carpets, and vendors arranged their wares. Mercy observed them all with new eyes, noticing patterns she'd never seen before.

A woman approached a fruit seller, her sleeve riding up as she reached for an apple. Mercy caught the quick flash of a blade, concealed but ready. The fruit seller's eyes narrowed, his hand moving beneath the counter. The woman retreated without a word.

"You see that?" a voice muttered near Mercy's ear, causing her to startle. An elderly woman with a basket of wilted flowers nodded toward the departing figure. "Always watch the hands, girl. Hands tell true intentions when faces lie."

Before Mercy could respond, the flower seller shuffled away, leaving only this fragment of street wisdom behind.

Throughout the morning, Mercy applied this lesson, studying the movements of those around her. The constable's deliberate stride as he patrolled Neal Street. The pickpocket's dancing fingers near the baker's shop. The charitable lady whose eyes never quite met those of the beggars she tossed pennies to.

By midday, Mercy had mapped the constables' routes in her mind. Every two hours, they passed the same corners, predictable as clockwork. Between their appearances, the street's character shifted subtly—children darted out from hiding places, vendors lowered prices on questionable goods, and the desperate emerged from shadows.

She kept to main thoroughfares, remembering whispered warnings about certain alleys. "Don't go down Black Lion Passage after dark," she'd heard a washerwoman tell her daughter. "And Neale's Yard belongs to the Butcher Boys—not actual butchers, mind, but they'll carve you just the same."

Her stomach cramped with hunger as she passed a pie seller whose wares sent steam rising into the cold air. Children no older than eight darted around his cart, one distracting him with questions while another filched a dropped crust from the ground.

"Spare a crust, mister?" A small girl with matted hair tugged at the vendor's apron.

"Off with you!" He swatted at her like an insect. "I've no charity for street rats."

The girl darted away, but not before Mercy noticed something clutched in her tiny fist—a whole meat pie, somehow spirited away during the exchange.

Mercy's mouth watered at the thought of warm food, but she turned away. Her mother's voice echoed in her mind: "Our hands were made for creating, not taking, Mercy."

Instead, she sat on a church step, watching street life unfold. A group of children played near an overturned cart, their laughter incongruous with their ragged appearance. Despite their obvious poverty, they seemed almost carefree, sharing some private joke as they huddled together.

One boy stood slightly apart, older than the rest. He directed their activities with casual authority, his sharp eyes constantly scanning the street. When a smaller child returned with half a loaf, the older boy broke it into portions, ensuring the youngest ate first.

Curious, Mercy edged closer, sheltering behind the cart. The children's chatter quieted as they noticed her presence.

"Who's she then?" whispered a freckled boy with a missing front tooth.

The leader turned, fixing Mercy with bright blue eyes that seemed to assess her worth in an instant. His light brown hair fell across his forehead as he tilted his head, considering her.

"New to the streets, ain't you?" he called out, neither hostile nor particularly welcoming. "Got that look about you."

Mercy clutched her sewing box tighter. "I'm just passing through."

The boy laughed, a surprisingly warm sound. "Nobody's just passing through Seven Dials, love. You're either running from something or looking for something." He approached with confident strides, stopping just beyond arm's reach. "Tommy's what they call me. Tommy Quick-Fingers to some."

As if to demonstrate the nickname's origin, his hand darted out in a blur of movement toward a distracted baker across the street. When he turned back to Mercy, a warm roll rested in his palm.

"Hungry?" He offered it to a tiny girl who had crept up beside him, her eyes wide with gratitude as she accepted the prize.

Tommy's gaze returned to Mercy, assessing the sewing box, her worn but clean dress, the careful way she held herself. "You look like you could use a friend," he said, producing another roll as if from thin air and extending it toward her. "Streets get cold when you're alone."

Mercy hesitated, her stomach twisting with hunger while her conscience pulled in the opposite direction. Tommy seemed to read her thoughts.

"Not stolen," he said with a wink. "Baker Hodges puts out the day-olds for us. He pretends not to notice so the other shopkeepers don't think him soft."

Tentatively, Mercy accepted the offering. "Thank you."

Over the next hour, Mercy observed the children's interactions. They operated with surprising organisation, each returning with contributions—pennies earned holding horses, scraps gathered from kitchens, information about which shops might need errands run. Everything went into a common pool, distributed according to need rather than contribution.

"That's Pip," Tommy explained, pointing to the freckled boy. "Best crossing-sweeper in London. And that's Mary and Little Jem—brother and sister. Parents died in the fever last year."

The children regarded Mercy with cautious curiosity, whispering among themselves until Tommy silenced them with a look.

"What can you do?" he asked Mercy directly.

She opened her sewing box in response, revealing neat spools of thread and gleaming needles.

Tommy's eyebrows rose. "Fancy. You a seamstress then?"

"My mother taught me." Mercy demonstrated by quickly mending a tear in Mary's shawl, her fingers working with practiced precision.

"Useful, that is," Tommy nodded approvingly. "People always needing mending."

As evening approached, Tommy gestured for Mercy to follow. "Got a place. Better than doorways."

The group wound through back streets, finally stopping at a seemingly abandoned warehouse. Tommy led them through a hidden entrance to a cellar below, where makeshift beds of straw and salvaged blankets created a surprisingly cozy refuge.

"Home sweet home," Tommy announced with a theatrical bow. "Not Buckingham Palace, but keeps the rain off."

In the dim light of a carefully tended candle stub, the children settled into their nightly routine. They shared the day's findings—half a loaf, some cheese rinds, an apple with only one bruised spot. Tommy ensured everyone received a portion, his own share no larger than the rest.

Later, as the younger children drifted to sleep, Tommy sat beside Mercy on a wooden crate.

"Why'd you help me?" she asked quietly.

Tommy shrugged. "Someone helped me once. Besides," his voice took on a matter-of-fact tone, "streets are safer when we stick together. You're one of us now—if you want to be."

For the first time since her mother's death, Mercy felt the faintest whisper of belonging. These children, forged into family by shared hardship, offered something she desperately needed: protection, purpose, perhaps even friendship.

"I'd like that," she whispered, her fingers still resting on her mother's sewing box—her past connected to this unexpected present.

Tommy nodded, satisfied. "Get some sleep then. Tomorrow's another day of honest work." His mouth quirked into a mischievous smile. "Mostly honest, anyway."

9
SLUMBER IN THE CELLAR

The cellar fell silent save for the soft breathing of slumbering children. Mercy sat awake, her back against the cold stone wall, moonlight filtering through a narrow crack above. She cradled her mother's sewing box in her lap, running her fingers along the worn edges, each scratch and dent a memory of Sarah Whitfield's hands.

She opened it carefully, mindful not to wake the others. Inside lay her mother's silver thimble, three precious needles, and spools of thread—tools that had once fed and clothed them. Now they represented possibility in this underground sanctuary.

"Each stitch is a prayer," her mother had said. Mercy wondered what prayer she might stitch now.

Across the cellar, Tommy slept with one arm protectively stretched toward little Mary. Beside them, Pip curled like a comma, his broom still clutched in grimy fingers. These children—so clever, so resilient—had fashioned a family from nothing but shared hardship and stubborn hope.

Mercy's fingers traced the Bible verse her mother had

carved into the box lid: "The Lord is my shepherd." The words felt different now, here among London's forgotten lambs.

Her thoughts wandered to the fine houses she'd visited with her mother, delivering embroidery to ladies who paid more for decorative handkerchiefs than these children saw in months. Such waste in those homes, such abundance. And here, children celebrated finding half a loaf of stale bread.

A plan began to form in Mercy's mind. Not just survival—something more. These children deserved warmth, safety, proper beds. They deserved to learn their letters and numbers, to have clean clothes and full bellies.

Perhaps her needle could build that bridge. Not immediately, but someday. She imagined a proper room with windows, a fire in the grate, these same children laughing around a table as she taught them to read from her mother's Bible.

Pip stirred in his sleep, muttering something about constables. Mercy tucked her box away and moved to adjust the thin blanket that had slipped from his shoulders.

She crept to the wall and peered through the crack. Outside, snow had begun to fall, silent white flakes drifting through lamplight. Beautiful and cold at once—like London itself.

Tomorrow would bring hunger and cold again. Tomorrow she would have to prove her worth to this makeshift family. But for now, watching the snow fall on a world that had both broken and saved her, Mercy allowed herself to believe that even in Seven Dials, God might still be watching.

10

THREAD AND FAITH

Morning light crept through the cracks of the warehouse cellar, casting thin golden beams across the dusty floor. Mercy had risen before the others, quietly gathering her few possessions. She found a discarded wooden crate in the corner and dragged it to where light pooled beneath the highest window.

"This will do," she whispered, brushing away cobwebs and splinters.

With reverent care, she opened her mother's sewing box. The tools inside represented her only inheritance and sole means of survival. Mercy arranged them on the makeshift table, positioning her work space to catch what little light filtered down.

Tommy stirred from his corner. "What're you about, then?"

"Setting up shop." She straightened her shoulders. "I need to earn my keep."

He scratched his head, hair sticking in all directions. "With sewing? Down here?"

"Not here. Out there." She nodded toward the ceiling, toward the streets above. "I'll find customers."

Tommy's doubtful expression said everything his lips didn't. Still, he helped her gather scraps of fabric from their collective findings—a torn handkerchief, bits of canvas, a frayed ribbon that might be repurposed.

"People on the streets don't have coin for mending," he warned.

Mercy threaded a needle, the motion as natural as breathing. "Then I'll find those who do."

Seven Dials hummed with its usual morning chaos as Mercy stepped into the sunlight. Market vendors shouted their wares, children darted between carts, and the smell of fresh bread mingled with less pleasant odours. She'd spent her whole life here, yet now viewed the streets with new eyes—the eyes of someone who called a cellar home.

She clutched her small collection of supplies wrapped in a clean scrap of cloth and approached a woman whose skirt hem dragged in the mud.

"Pardon me, ma'am." Mercy's voice sounded thin against the market's roar. "I could mend that for you. A quick stitch would save the fabric."

The woman hurried past without acknowledging her.

Mercy tried again with an elderly man whose coat sleeve hung by threads. "Sir, I could repair that sleeve proper. Just a few pennies."

"Out of my way, beggar girl," he muttered, pushing past.

By midday, Mercy had approached fifteen potential customers without success. Her throat felt raw from shouting over the din, and her empty stomach twisted painfully. She leaned against a wall, fighting disappointment.

"Not giving up already, are you?"

She turned to find Tommy watching her, his quick fingers wrapped around an apple core he'd scavenged.

"Nobody wants mending from a street girl," she admitted.

Tommy took a final bite of his meagre find and tossed the remains to a grateful sparrow. "Try the shops instead. Shopkeepers know everybody. One good word from them's worth twenty of your own."

Mercy nodded, gathering her resolve. She approached Harding's Haberdashery, where her mother had occasionally purchased thread. Mr Harding glanced up from his ledger as the bell above the door announced her entrance.

Recognition flickered across his weathered face. "Sarah Whitfield's girl, aren't you?"

"Yes, sir." Hope fluttered in her chest. "I'm offering mending services now."

He studied her threadbare dress and tangled hair. Something softened in his expression.

"I've buttons need sewing on these shirts." He gestured to a stack of men's garments. "Can't sell them as is. Sixpence if you can manage them all by tomorrow."

Mercy's hands trembled as she accepted the work. "Thank you, Mr Harding. They'll be perfect, I promise."

Three more shopkeepers offered similar arrangements— small mending jobs paid in pennies or, from the baker's wife, a half-loaf of yesterday's bread. By evening, Mercy's fingers ached from hours of careful stitching, but pride warmed her chest as she counted her earnings.

Five precious pennies. Barely enough for tomorrow, and nothing for saving.

At the thread merchant's stall, Mercy hesitated between food and supplies. Her stomach growled its opinion, but her mind calculated differently. Without thread, there would be no work tomorrow.

"The black and the white," she decided, handing over three pennies. The merchant measured out modest lengths of each, nowhere near a full spool.

Hunger gnawed as she made her way back to the cellar, the remaining two pennies heavy in her pocket. She passed a fruit seller packing away his bruised wares and spent her final coins on three small, spotted apples—one for herself and two for the youngest children.

Night had fallen by the time she descended the cellar steps. The children gathered around as she distributed her meagre offerings, their eyes wide with gratitude that made her own hunger easier to bear.

When the others settled for sleep, Mercy positioned herself near the crack in the wall where faint moonlight seeped through. She opened her mother's Bible, the pages soft and familiar beneath her fingertips.

"The Lord is my shepherd; I shall not want," she read in a whisper. "He maketh me to lie down in green pastures: he leadeth me beside the still waters."

"What good's all that reading?" Pip's voice startled her. The boy watched from his pallet, eyes reflecting the moonlight. "God don't come to Seven Dials."

"He's everywhere," Mercy replied softly. "Even here."

"Then why're we hungry?" Another voice joined in—Mary this time.

Mercy closed the Bible, considering. "My mother always said faith isn't about having everything you want. It's about finding strength when you have nothing."

Her words hung in the damp air.

"Load of rubbish," muttered an older boy from the shadows.

Days passed in similar fashion. Mercy rose early, sought work throughout Seven Dials, and returned with whatever small earnings she managed. Some days brought relative success—a sixpence for repairing a tavern-keeper's linens. Others yielded nothing but tired feet and an empty stomach.

The children's initial mockery stung, but Mercy weathered it without complaint. "Praying won't fill your belly," they'd jeer when she read from her Bible. "Your God's forgotten about Seven Dials."

Everything changed the day little Mary fell ill. The child's forehead burned with fever, her thin frame wracked with coughing. Tommy brought water, but Mary couldn't keep it down.

That night, Mercy tore one of her precious clean rags into strips, soaking them in cool water to place on Mary's forehead. She sat beside the child through the darkness, murmuring prayers and stories to distract from the pain.

When morning came, Mercy divided her only crust of bread and offered it to Mary. The child managed a few bites before falling back into fitful sleep.

"You need that more than she does," Tommy observed, watching Mercy's trembling hands. "She might not last anyway."

"Every life matters," Mercy replied, remembering her mother's words. "If God notices when a sparrow falls, we should notice too."

She missed a full day of work tending to Mary. By evening, her own hunger made her dizzy, but the child's fever had broken. Mercy slumped against the wall, exhaustion claiming her as the others returned from their day's scavenging.

She awoke to something pressed into her hand—half an apple, a chunk of cheese, a slightly stale roll.

"Eat," Tommy instructed. Behind him stood the other children, even those who had mocked her faith the loudest.

"We saved you portions," Pip explained awkwardly. "Since you saved Mary."

Mercy's vision blurred with tears as she accepted their offerings. Not mockery now, but a different light shone in their eyes—the cautious respect that comes from witnessing quiet strength.

"Thank you," she whispered, breaking the bread to share despite their protests.

In that moment, hungry and tired in a damp cellar beneath Seven Dials, Mercy felt her mother's presence as clearly as if Sarah sat beside her. Each stitch is a prayer, she'd said. Each kindness, a testament of faith.

11

THREADS OF CONNECTION

"Run!" Tommy's voice cut through the market din. Mercy's fingers closed around little Mary's hand as they darted between stalls. Behind them, the pie seller bellowed accusations, his face purple with rage. "Thieves! Stop those gutter rats!"

"This way," Mercy hissed, pulling the children toward the narrow alley behind the chandler's shop. Her heart hammered against her ribs as heavy footsteps pounded the cobblestones behind them.

She hadn't stolen anything—none of them had. The pie had fallen from a customer's hand, and Tommy had simply reached for it. But the seller's missing inventory from earlier thefts made him quick to blame the ragged children.

"The constable's coming," Pip warned, his voice tight with fear.

Mercy surveyed their small group—five children with nowhere to hide. Her gaze landed on a stack of empty crates beside the back entrance of a milliner's shop.

"Quick, behind these. Mary, under my skirt."

They huddled together, breaths shallow, as the constable's boots appeared at the alley entrance. Mary trembled against Mercy's legs, her tiny fingers digging into the worn fabric of Mercy's skirt.

"I saw nothing, sir," came the voice of the milliner's assistant, sweeping the back step. "Just me out here."

The constable grunted and moved on. Only when his footsteps faded did Mercy exhale.

"That was too close," Tommy muttered, helping little Nell from behind the crates.

"We need to be more careful," Mercy replied, straightening Mary's tattered cap. "They're watching us closer these days."

Later that night, while the others slept, Mercy sat with her Bible open on her lap. The candle stub Tommy had found cast just enough light to read by. Her fingers traced familiar verses, finding comfort in their constancy when everything else felt uncertain.

She glanced at the sleeping children—Tommy curled protectively around Pip, Mary and Nell huddled together for warmth, Jack snoring softly in the corner. Something had shifted in their attitudes toward her these past weeks. The mockery had given way to respect, then to something warmer that reminded her of family.

"Your mother would be proud," Tommy's voice startled her. He sat up, rubbing sleep from his eyes.

Mercy closed the Bible. "I hope so."

"She would. You've got all of us listening for God now, haven't you?" He gestured toward Mary, who insisted on prayers before sleep. "Even Jack asks for blessings, though he'd never admit it."

Mercy smiled, warmth spreading through her chest despite

the cellar's chill. "We take care of each other. That's what matters."

The next evening brought unexpected fortune—Tommy had helped a baker unload his cart and received half a loaf as payment. They gathered around their makeshift table—a discarded crate—breaking bread with the ceremony of a feast.

"To Mercy," Jack raised his crust, "for mending my coat so I didn't freeze last week."

"To Tommy," Pip chimed in, "for the bread."

"To all of us," Mercy added softly, "for finding each other."

They shared stories as they ate—Tommy's adventures running errands, Nell's discovery of a lost hairpin she'd polished to gleaming, Jack's proud recounting of the Bible verse Mercy had taught him.

In these moments, the cellar transformed. No longer merely shelter, but home. Not just a gathering of orphans, but family.

The next afternoon, Mercy sat cross-legged near the cellar's lone window, where weak sunlight filtered through. She worked on a small coat fashioned from discarded fabric scraps, each stitch neat despite the poor light.

"Is that for me?" Mary asked, peering over her shoulder.

"Just in time for winter," Mercy nodded, holding it up. The patchwork of blues and browns formed an unexpectedly beautiful pattern.

Mary's eyes widened. "It's the prettiest thing I've ever seen."

As the child skipped away to show the others, Mercy continued her work, the familiar rhythm of needle and thread connecting her to her mother's memory. Behind her, children's laughter echoed off stone walls, no longer hollow with desperation but bright with belonging.

Faith, Mercy thought, worked itself out in unexpected ways. Not in grand churches or fine homes, but here—in shared bread, mended clothes, and the family they'd built from nothing but trust and care.

12

WINTER'S RETURN

The snow fell in thick, relentless sheets, transforming Seven Dials into a treacherous maze of white. Mercy pulled her threadbare shawl tighter around her shoulders, the biting wind finding every hole in the worn fabric. A year had passed since her mother's death—a full turning of seasons that had brought her from daughter to orphan to this strange position as mother-figure to a band of street children.

This winter cut deeper than the last. Perhaps because she no longer had the shelter of four walls, or perhaps because grief had hollowed something vital inside her.

"Just a bit further," she murmured to herself, stumbling slightly as a cough racked her thin frame. The spasm lasted longer this time, leaving her gasping against a lamppost, her breath forming desperate clouds in the frigid air.

She'd been fighting this cough for weeks now. At first, just a tickle in her throat that she could ignore while mending Mr Harding's shirts or teaching Mary her letters. But the cold had settled in her chest, a persistent ache that worsened with each passing day.

The parcel of mending tucked beneath her arm felt impossibly heavy. Three pennies' worth of work—barely enough for bread, let alone the medicine the apothecary had suggested when she'd inquired about her symptoms. She couldn't afford to rest. Tommy brought what he could, but winter made everyone desperate, and charity dried up like puddles in summer heat.

Another coughing fit doubled her over. When she straightened, black spots danced before her eyes.

"God, give me strength," she whispered, her mother's favourite prayer. "Just until I reach the children."

By the time Mercy descended the cellar steps, her legs trembled beneath her. The familiar smell of damp stone and unwashed bodies greeted her, along with Mary's delighted cry.

"Mercy's back!"

Tiny arms wrapped around her waist. Mercy forced a smile, though her face felt wooden, too hot and too cold all at once.

"Did you bring thread?" Mary asked, eyes bright with hope.

"Better. Bread." Mercy produced the small loaf she'd purchased with one of her precious pennies. "And look—the baker's wife gave me these scraps for patching."

The woollen bits would make decent patches for Jack's torn trousers. If her fingers would just stop shaking long enough to thread the needle.

"You don't look right," Tommy observed, his voice low as the younger children divided the bread. "You're pale as churchyard stone."

"I'm fine," Mercy insisted, settling at her corner where a crate served as her workbench. "Just tired from the cold."

But she wasn't fine. The needle slipped from her fingers three times before she managed to thread it. The stitches she produced wavered drunkenly across the fabric. When had sewing become so difficult? Her mother had praised her steady hand, her even stitches. Now the simplest darn defeated her.

Night fell, bringing no relief from the cold. Mercy's skin burned while her bones seemed carved from ice. She'd managed two small repairs before her body betrayed her completely, the needle falling from nerveless fingers as sweat beaded her brow.

"You need to lie down," Tommy insisted, taking the mending from her lap.

She didn't protest. Her head swam, thoughts tangling like loose thread.

The makeshift bed of rags provided little comfort. Around her, the children settled for the night, their breathing a chorus that should have been soothing. Instead, each inhalation reminded Mercy of her mother's final, rattling breaths.

Had it truly been a year? The grief felt fresh as an open wound.

Staring at the ceiling, where moisture gathered in glistening beads, Mercy confronted the thought she'd been pushing away for days: she was following her mother into illness, perhaps into death.

"Are you there?" she whispered, the words meant for ears beyond the cellar walls. "Have you forgotten me?"

The silence that answered seemed heavy with accusation. What had become of the faith that sustained her through those first terrible days of homelessness? What good were prayers that went unanswered while children starved and froze?

Mary coughed in her sleep, a small echo of Mercy's own affliction. Tommy had wrapped his own blanket around the child, sacrificing his comfort for hers just as Mercy had taught them. They looked after each other now.

But who would look after them if she couldn't rise tomorrow? If her fever worsened? If she slipped away like her mother, leaving only memories and an old sewing box?

The thought brought a surge of panic, then a wave of surrender. She was so tired. So very tired of fighting each day for scraps, of stretching pennies and fabric and hope until all three threatened to snap.

"I don't know if I can keep going," she admitted to the darkness. Her mother's face swam before her closed eyes—not as she'd looked in death, but vibrant and loving, teaching Mercy to create beauty from nothing.

The memory brought no comfort tonight, only a hollowness that expanded with each laboured breath.

13
COLLAPSE

Morning brought no relief. Mercy's head throbbed with each heartbeat, her throat raw from coughing through the night. She struggled to rise, limbs heavy as lead weights.

"You shouldn't be up," Tommy said, pressing a chipped cup of water into her trembling hands. "Jack can deliver your mending."

"No." The word scraped against her throat. "Mrs Beau pays only to me. She doesn't trust children she doesn't know."

Mercy didn't mention the real reason—that Mrs Beau's payment would come in the form of a woollen shawl rather than coins. Something they desperately needed, with snow falling thicker each hour.

By midday, Mercy had managed to drag herself to Mrs Beau's townhouse, deliver the mending, and collect the promised shawl. The effort cost her dearly. Each step back through Seven Dials felt like wading through treacle, her body alternating between burning heat and bone-deep chills.

The snow began falling harder, driven by a bitter wind that

sliced through her thin dress. Darkness came early, street lamps creating hazy globes in the swirling white. Mercy tucked the precious shawl inside her coat, saving it for Mary and the younger children.

"Just a bit further," she murmured, though the warehouse cellar seemed impossibly distant.

A violent coughing fit doubled her over. When she straightened, the street tilted alarmingly. Which way had she been heading? The familiar landmarks of Seven Dials blurred together, transformed by snow into an alien landscape.

She stumbled forward, one hand pressed against buildings to keep herself upright. The wind howled down the narrow streets, driving icy needles into her exposed skin.

"Mother," she whispered, "I don't know the way."

Her feet moved without direction, each step more uncertain than the last. When the spire of St Dunstan's Church appeared through the snowfall, relief flooded through her. Not home, but shelter at least.

The church doors would be locked, but the deep doorway might offer some protection from the wind until her head cleared. Just a brief rest, then she'd find her way back to the children.

Mercy's vision narrowed to that single destination—the stone archway promising respite. Her mother's voice seemed to whisper encouragement, though whether memory or delirium, she couldn't tell.

"Keep going, my love. Just a few more steps."

The sewing box clutched against her chest grew impossibly heavy. She wouldn't let it go—couldn't abandon the last piece of her mother, even as her fingers grew numb and clumsy.

Snow accumulated on her shoulders, melting against her fever-hot skin. The church wavered before her, appearing close then impossibly far, like something viewed through disturbed water.

"God notices every sparrow that falls." Her mother's words floated through her mind. *"How much more does He care for you?"*

"Then why am I alone?" Mercy whispered, tasting salt and realising she was crying. "Why did He take you from me?"

No answer came, only the howling wind and the soft hiss of falling snow.

The stone steps of St Dunstan's loomed before her suddenly. She'd made it. Just three steps up to the sheltered doorway. Mercy lifted her foot, but her leg buckled beneath her weight.

She fell forward, the sewing box tumbling from her grasp. Precious needles and thread scattered across the snow-covered stone. With the last of her strength, Mercy lunged for the box, gathering it back into her arms. She did her best to retrieve as many as she could.

The world tilted, darkness encroaching at the edges of her vision. She crawled the final distance to the doorway, collapsing against the heavy wooden door. The meagre shelter did little to block the wind, but Mercy lacked the strength to move further.

Her thoughts scattered like the contents of her sewing box had, and just as with her previous tools, she did her best to gather them back together. The children waiting for her. Tommy would look after them tonight. The warehouse cellar seemed a world away now.

The silver thimble pressed against her palm, its familiar shape a small comfort. She should get up. Continue on. Find her way home.

But her body refused to obey, limbs leaden with exhaustion and illness. The snow continued to fall, dusting her huddled form with white. The cold no longer bothered her, replaced by a dangerous warmth spreading through her limbs.

"I'm sorry," she whispered, unsure if she addressed her mother, God, or the children she'd failed to return to.

Mercy's eyes drifted closed, her breathing shallow. The sewing box clutched against her chest rose and fell with each laboured breath. Darkness beckoned, promising an end to pain, to struggle, to the constant battle for survival.

She didn't hear the footsteps approaching through the snow.

14
FATHER MCKINNON

F ather Benedict McKinnon hurried through the snowstorm, his shoulders hunched against the biting wind. The meeting with the Widow Hartley had run longer than expected, her grief still raw six months after her husband's passing. He'd promised to check on her again tomorrow, though the weather made all plans uncertain.

The snow-laden streets of Seven Dials lay eerily quiet, most sensible souls tucked away indoors. Benedict's thoughts drifted to his warm rectory as he approached St Dunstan's Church, eager for a cup of tea and the small fire waiting in his study.

He nearly missed the huddled shape in the doorway.

"Good Heavens," he murmured, squinting through the swirling snow. The bundle shifted slightly—a person, not discarded rubbish.

Benedict rushed forward, his heart quickening. A girl lay crumpled against the heavy oak door, snow already forming a thin blanket over her still form. Her face, flushed with fever, stood in stark contrast to her blue-tinged lips.

"Child?" He knelt beside her, brushing snow from her face. "Can you hear me?"

No response came, though her chest rose and fell with shallow breaths. She clutched something to her chest—a wooden box of some kind. Her skin burned beneath his touch despite the freezing air.

"You poor soul," Benedict whispered, shrugging off his heavy coat to wrap around her frail shoulders. "What's brought you to God's doorstep tonight?"

He glanced around the empty street. No help would come from that quarter. The girl needed warmth, medicine, and care —immediately.

"You're not spending another moment in this cold," he declared, though she couldn't hear him.

Benedict slipped his arms beneath her slight frame, careful not to disturb whatever she held so preciously. She weighed hardly anything at all, her body burning with fever against his chest as he lifted her.

"Mrs Campbell," he called, pushing through the side door that led to the vestry. "Mrs Campbell, we need help!"

His housekeeper appeared, eyes widening at the sight.

"Father, what have you found?"

"A child dying of fever on our doorstep. Quick—prepare a pallet by the fire and fetch Dr Morgan."

Mrs Campbell hesitated. "The doctor won't come to Seven Dials in this weather, and we've no space—"

"Then I'll give her my bed," Benedict insisted. "And if Morgan won't come, I'll go to him. No soul seeking shelter at God's house will be turned away tonight."

15
FEVER

Warmth. That was the first sensation Mercy felt as she drifted between worlds. Not the false, dangerous warmth of freezing to death in the snow, but true, nurturing heat that seemed to reach deep into her bones. Soft blankets enveloped her, and somewhere beyond her consciousness, a gentle Irish lilt murmured words she couldn't quite grasp.

"That's it, child. Rest now." A cool cloth pressed against her forehead. "Mrs Campbell, another blanket, if you please. She's burning with fever."

Mercy's eyes fluttered open briefly, taking in unfamiliar stone walls that glowed orange in firelight. She tried to speak, but her throat seized with coughing that tore through her chest like knives.

"Easy now." Strong hands lifted her shoulders, helping her sit upright enough to breathe. "Small sips only."

Water touched her parched lips. Mercy drank greedily until another coughing fit overtook her.

"My ... box," she whispered when she could finally speak.

"It's here, safe beside you." The kind-eyed priest placed her mother's sewing box within reach of her trembling fingers. "I wouldn't separate you from something so precious."

Relief washed over her as her fingertips traced the familiar wood grain before darkness claimed her again.

"My name is Father Benedict McKinnon. You are safe now."

Through the fever dreams, Scripture flowed around her like a river. The priest's voice became her anchor as he read by candlelight.

"Even youths grow tired and weary, and young men stumble and fall; but those who hope in the Lord will renew their strength. They will soar on wings like eagles; they will run and not grow weary; they will walk and not be faint."

The words wrapped around her like the blankets, holding her safe from the abyss that threatened to claim her. Sometimes she imagined it was her mother's voice reading, but then the Irish accent would return, grounding her to this strange new reality.

"Tommy," she mumbled during one moment of clarity. "The children ..."

"Shh, focus on healing first," the priest soothed. "God sees the children, just as He saw you at our door."

Days blurred together in a haze of fever and coughing. Sometimes Mercy woke to find an elderly woman spooning broth between her lips. Other times, the priest sat beside her bed, reading or praying quietly.

"I don't want to be alone again," she whispered one night, tears streaming down her face. "Mother said God would provide, but I was so cold, so hungry ..."

"And yet, here you are." The priest's hand found hers. "Not abandoned after all."

16

AWAKE

When consciousness finally settled upon Mercy like morning dew, she opened her eyes to find Father McKinnon stirring a pot of broth by the small fireplace in the vestry.

His cassock sleeves were rolled up to his elbows, revealing forearms knotted with lean muscle. The room smelled of herbs and wood smoke. He hummed softly—a hymn Mercy half-remembered — as he ladled steaming broth into a wooden bowl.

Turning, he caught her watching and his face brightened. "Ah, you've returned to us properly this time. Thanks be to God." He crossed the small room in three strides, setting the bowl aside to press his palm against her forehead. His brow furrowed. "Still warm, but better than yesterday. You've had us worried, Miss ..."

"Mercy," she whispered, her voice cracking from disuse. "Mercy Whitfield."

"A fitting name." He offered the broth, supporting her as

she struggled to sit. "Small sips now, Miss Whitfield. You've been lost to fever for nearly a week."

Mercy's hand trembled as she gripped the spoon. A week? The children would think she'd abandoned them. Tommy would be looking for her. She took a careful sip of broth, the simple flavour exploding across her tongue. Her hollow stomach growled painfully.

"My sewing box—"

"Safe beside your bed, as promised." Father McKinnon nodded toward the wooden box tucked beside her makeshift pallet. "You clutched it even in fever. Must be precious indeed."

"It was my mother's." Mercy's fingers traced the familiar wood grain. "It's all I have left of her. Well, that and her Bible."

"And her teachings, I'd wager." The priest settled onto a stool beside her bed. "You spoke of her often in your fever. Sarah, was it?"

Mercy nodded, a lump forming in her throat. "She taught me everything. How to read, to pray. How to survive." Her fingers flipped open the box lid, revealing spools of thread, needles, and her mother's silver thimble. Mercy was relieved she hadn't lost the thimble when everything had been scattered. "She was the finest seamstress in Seven Dials. Taught me every stitch she knew."

Father McKinnon leaned forward, genuine interest lighting his deep brown eyes. "You're a seamstress too, then?"

"Yes." Pride straightened Mercy's shoulders despite her weakness. "I took in mending after Mother died. Fixed tears, hemmed skirts, mended holes for anyone who could spare a penny."

"While living on the streets?" Disbelief coloured his tone.

Mercy sipped more broth before answering. "I had a room with Mother, above the cobbler's shop. After she died, I couldn't pay the rent." The memory of Mr Edwards's cold dismissal still stung. "Then I met Tommy and the other children. We looked after each other."

"And now you'll be looked after here, until you're well enough to stand on your own two feet." Father McKinnon's voice held such certainty that Mercy couldn't help but believe him. "The vestry isn't much, but it's warm and dry. You'll be safe here."

"I couldn't impose—"

"Nonsense." He waved away her protest. "Christ teaches us to shelter the stranger. You're no longer a stranger, Miss Whitfield, but you certainly need shelter."

Before Mercy could respond, the door swung open, admitting a blast of cold air and a short, plump woman with steel-grey hair bundled beneath a woollen cap. She carried a basket over one arm and wore a practical dark dress beneath a thick shawl.

"Ah, she's awake at last!" The woman bustled forward, her light blue eyes twinkling with warmth despite her brisk manner. "About time too. I've been warming this stone jar for naught these three days." A soft Scottish lilt coloured her words.

"Mercy Whitfield, meet Mrs Morag Campbell, who keeps both this church and me in working order." Father McKinnon stood, taking the basket from the older woman's arm. "Without her, I fear both would fall to ruin."

"Aye, and don't you forget it." Mrs Campbell placed a warm stone jar wrapped in flannel at Mercy's feet, then pressed weathered palms against Mercy's cheeks, assessing her. "Still feverish, but the worst has passed. Ye've the look of a fighter about ye, lass."

Despite her weakened state, Mercy couldn't help smiling at the woman's forthright manner. "Thank you for helping care for me, Mrs Campbell."

"Pah, what else would we do? Leave ye to freeze on the doorstep?" She adjusted Mercy's blankets with practised efficiency. "Fresh linens tomorrow, and perhaps a proper bath if the fever's truly broken. I've brought more broth, and bread too —though mind ye go slowly. Your stomach will be tender after such illness."

17

MRS CAMPBELL

Over the following days, as Mercy's strength gradually returned, she found herself increasingly drawn to Mrs Campbell's practical wisdom and no-nonsense affection. The Scottish woman appeared each morning with fresh linens or food, staying to share stories while she taught Mercy how to maintain the vestry.

"Ye've got deft hands," Mrs Campbell observed as Mercy darned a hole in one of the altar cloths. "Your stitches are finer than any I've seen."

"Mother always said each stitch should be invisible to all but God," Mercy replied, her needle flashing in the afternoon light.

"Wise woman, your mother." Mrs Campbell nodded approvingly. "You'll find prayer and a good stitch can mend a multitude of woes, lass."

The rhythmic motion of sewing soothed Mercy's troubled thoughts about Tommy and the children. Each pull of thread through fabric felt like drawing her scattered self, back together. Under Mrs Campbell's watchful eye, she learned to manage the small vestry, to bank coals properly, to wash linens until they gleamed.

"I was not always a housekeeper, ye know," Mrs Campbell confided one afternoon as they folded fresh linen. "I had a fine home once, in the highlands. A husband who loved me, and a daughter of my own."

Mercy looked up, surprised. "What happened?"

"Life happened, lass." Sadness briefly shadowed the older woman's face. "The fever took my Robert and my sweet Fiona in one cruel winter. But God never abandons His children, even when the path grows dark." She smoothed the linen with gnarled fingers. "I found my way to London, to this church. Found purpose again."

"My mother said something similar before she died," Mercy whispered. "That God would provide, even when I couldn't see the path forward."

"Smart woman, your mother." Mrs Campbell patted Mercy's hand. "And look—here ye are, safe and healing. The path continues, even through the darkest valley."

18

A FAMILIAR FACE

One bright afternoon, Mercy sat curled on her pallet, her mother's Bible open on her lap. The weak sunlight streamed through the vestry's narrow window, casting a golden glow across the pages. After a morning of sweeping and dusting—tasks Mrs Campbell insisted would help rebuild her strength—Mercy savoured this moment of quiet reflection.

A sharp, distinctive rap at the door pulled her from her reading. Her heart quickened with recognition. That pattern— three quick taps followed by two slower ones—belonged to only one person. She scrambled to her feet, crossed the stone floor, and pulled open the heavy door.

"Tommy!"

There he stood, cap in hand, his blue eyes bright with mischief and relief. A grin split his face, transforming his usually wary expression into something boyish and carefree.

"Thought you'd gone and died on us," he said, though the tremor in his voice betrayed his concern. "Looked everywhere for days."

Mercy pulled him inside, overcome with joy at seeing a face from her other life. "You found me."

"Course I did. I'm Quick-Fingers, ain't I? Best finder in Seven Dials." Tommy reached into his jacket and produced a small parcel wrapped in newspaper. "Brought you something."

Mercy unwrapped it carefully. Inside lay a chunk of crusty bread and something truly miraculous—a small honey cake, still warm and fragrant.

"Where on earth did you get this?" She breathed in the sweet scent, memories of rare childhood treats washing over her.

Tommy shrugged, attempting nonchalance despite his evident pride. "Baker Simmons lets me sweep his shop now. Gives me bits and bobs what can't be sold. Said this one burnt on the edge, but it looks proper fine to me."

They shared the treasure, sitting together on the pallet as Tommy filled her in on the children's adventures. Little Mary had found a brass button she swore was pure gold. Pip had mastered a new street crossing and earned three whole pennies in one day from gentlemen grateful for clean boots.

"And Billy?" Mercy asked, laughing as Tommy described the youngest boy's misadventure with a stray cat.

"Still asking when you're coming back," Tommy answered, brushing crumbs from his coat. "They all do."

The vestry rang with their laughter, so different from the hollow echoes of their warehouse cellar. Mercy watched Tommy's animated gestures, his hands painting pictures in the air as he spoke. How strange that just weeks ago, she'd been certain God had abandoned her. Yet here she sat, warm and healing, with friends who sought her out and people who cared for her recovery.

"They're all right, then? Truly?" She needed to know.

"Right as rain," Tommy nodded. "Found a better spot for

sleeping—old stable with half a roof. Drier than the cellar, at least. And I've been teaching the little ones what you showed me about finding honest work."

Pride swelled in Mercy's chest. Despite her absence, something good remained. The seeds of care she'd planted continued to grow.

"Father McKinnon says I'm to stay until I'm properly well," she told him. "But I won't forget you all. I promise."

Tommy nudged her shoulder gently. "I know you won't. You're not the forgetting kind."

As the afternoon light began to fade, Mercy marvelled at how her world had expanded. The desperate girl who'd collapsed in the snow had found more than shelter within these stone walls. She'd found kindness in Mrs Campbell's practical wisdom, compassion in Father McKinnon's quiet faith, and now the loyalty of Tommy's unexpected visit.

Perhaps her mother had been right after all. God did notice when sparrows fell—and sometimes sent unlikely angels to catch them.

19
AN OPPORTUNITY

The first daffodils peeked through the cracked stones in St Dunstan's garden, their bright yellow faces turned toward the strengthening sun. Mercy paused in her sweeping to watch a robin hop between the headstones, its red breast vivid against the weathered grey. Spring had crept into London almost without her noticing, bringing with it a gentle warmth that seemed to thaw something frozen inside her chest.

She trailed her fingers along the stone wall as she made her way back to the vestry, feeling the rough texture catch against her calluses. The fever had left her weaker than she'd expected, but each day brought new strength to her limbs. Mrs Campbell insisted that fresh air would put colour back in her cheeks, though Mercy suspected the old woman simply wanted her to experience the resurrection happening in the garden—life returning after the bitter cold, just as Mercy herself was returning to the land of the living.

Through the vestry window, sunlight spilled across her pallet in a golden pool. Mercy stood in its warmth, closing her eyes to feel it on her face. How different from the harsh winter light that had illuminated her mother's final days or the cold moonlight that had guided her through Seven Dials' treacherous alleys. This light felt like a promise.

"There you are, lass." Mrs Campbell bustled in, arms laden with a covered pot that released tantalising aromas. "Father McKinnon's finishing up with old Mr Watson, but he'll be joining us shortly for our supper."

Mercy hurried to help, taking the pot and setting it on the small table they'd assembled from crates. "It smells wonderful."

"My grandmother's Scotch broth," Mrs Campbell said proudly, producing a loaf of bread from her basket. "Nothing better for putting flesh on bones that need it."

Father McKinnon arrived as they finished setting out the simple meal, his face lighting up at the domestic scene before him. "What's this then? A feast?"

"Hardly a feast," Mrs Campbell snorted, but her eyes twinkled with pleasure. "Just something to warm us on this fine evening."

They gathered around the makeshift table, shoulders touching in the small space. Father McKinnon said grace, his Irish lilt wrapping the familiar words in music. Mercy bowed her head, feeling strangely at home in this odd assemblage—a Scottish housekeeper, an Irish priest, and a girl from Seven Dials breaking bread together as if they belonged to each other.

"This reminds me of my mother's cooking," Mercy said after her first spoonful of the rich broth.

"Does it now?" Mrs Campbell looked pleased. "Tell us about her."

The invitation opened a floodgate. Mercy found herself sharing memories she'd kept locked away—her mother's gentle hands guiding her own through complicated stitches, the way she'd sing hymns while they worked, how she could create beauty from the simplest materials.

Father McKinnon shared stories of his childhood in County Kerry, mimicking his own mother's voice as she scolded him for bringing frogs into the kitchen. Mrs Campbell countered with tales of highland winters so fierce that sheep would huddle against their cottage door for warmth.

Laughter flowed as freely as the weak tea they shared after the meal. In that moment, the vestry felt neither like a temporary shelter nor a charity, but something closer to home.

"I've been meaning to speak with you," Father McKinnon said as they cleared away the dishes. "About your future."

Mercy's hands stilled on the cloth she'd been using to dry a bowl. "My future?"

"You've recovered well," he said, his voice gentle. "And while you're welcome to stay as long as needed, I wonder if you might be ready for something more permanent."

Mrs Campbell nodded encouragingly, taking the dried bowl from Mercy's hands.

"I've been speaking with some of my parishioners," Father McKinnon continued. "People of means who might offer positions in their households."

"A position?" Mercy whispered, hardly daring to hope. "As a seamstress?"

"Perhaps eventually," he said. "But to start, as an under-housemaid in a good family. One that would value your skills and treat you with respect."

Mrs Campbell patted Mercy's hand. "A proper position in a grand house would be a fine start for a girl with your talents."

"There's a family—the Belmonts of Belgrave Square," Father McKinnon explained. "Master Charles is a textile merchant of excellent reputation. His wife, Lady Elizabeth, serves on several charitable committees. They're known to be fair and kind to their staff."

Mercy's heart quickened. "Belgrave Square?" The name itself conjured images of grand houses with polished brass knockers and pristine white steps—a world away from Seven Dials.

"Mrs Marsh, their housekeeper, mentioned they need an under-housemaid. When I spoke of your needlework skills, she seemed most interested." His eyes crinkled with the warmth of his smile. "It would be a chance to build a life, Mercy. A respectable position with people who would appreciate your character as well as your work."

The spring sunshine continued to pool on the stone floor, and in its glow, Mercy could almost see a path forming— leading away from hunger and fear toward something solid and secure. Not just survival, but a life with possibility.

"Do you think I could?" she asked, her voice small but steady.

"I know you can," Father McKinnon said firmly. "God doesn't bring us through trials without purpose. Perhaps this is yours."

20

THE INTERVIEW

The following day dawned bright, but Mercy hardly noticed the cheerful weather as she paced the stone floor of the vestry.

"For Heaven's sake, child, you'll wear a groove in the stones," Mrs Campbell chuckled, entering with a basin of warm water. "Here now, let's wash your face proper. Can't have you meeting fine folk with smudges."

Mercy submitted to Mrs Campbell's ministrations, grateful for the older woman's steadying presence. For three days, they had been preparing for this moment—her interview with the Belmonts.

"Now, when you enter a room with your betters present, you curtsy like so." Mrs Campbell demonstrated, her knees creaking slightly as she dipped down with surprising grace. "Not too deep—you're not at court—but respectful, like."

Mercy attempted to mirror the movement, wobbling slightly.

"Again," Mrs Campbell instructed. "And keep your eyes down until spoken to."

They practiced until Mercy's legs ached, moving on to proper forms of address and the right responses to common questions. When Mercy fumbled over whether to call the lady of the house "ma'am" or "my lady," Mrs Campbell's stern expression dissolved into warm laughter.

"Oh, lass, the look on your face! As if you're facing the gallows instead of good fortune."

Mercy couldn't help but join in the laughter, tension draining from her shoulders. "I just want everything to be perfect."

"Perfect isn't what they're after. It's honest work and a willing heart." Mrs Campbell brushed imaginary lint from Mercy's sleeve. "Which you have in abundance."

The morning of the interview arrived with a flutter of nerves in Mercy's stomach. Mrs Campbell had gifted her a dress—one of her own from younger days, altered and mended with Mercy's expert stitches until it looked almost new. The grey wool was respectable, if plain, and Mrs Campbell insisted it showed Mercy's sensible nature.

Father McKinnon blessed her before she left, his Irish lilt warm with encouragement. "Remember, Mercy—God brought you to our doorstep for a reason. Trust in His path for you."

Clutching the precious letter of introduction, Mercy set out from Seven Dials toward Belgrave Square. With each step, the buildings around her grew grander, the streets wider and cleaner. Women in fine dresses strolled with parasols. Carriages rolled past with liveried footmen perched behind.

Mercy had visited wealthy areas before with her mother, delivering finished work to fine houses. But today was different. Today, she walked these streets not as a visitor but as someone who might belong here—in service, yes, but with purpose and place.

When Belgrave Square came into view, Mercy faltered

momentarily. The houses stood like palaces, their white facades gleaming in the spring sunshine. Iron railings surrounded pristine front gardens where early flowers nodded in neat beds.

"Number seventeen," she whispered to herself, counting along the magnificent buildings until she stood before the Belmont residence.

The brass knocker felt cool and heavy in her hand. After taking a deep breath, she rapped firmly against the polished black door.

A young footman answered, his livery impeccable. "Yes?"

"Mercy Whitfield, here to see Mrs Marsh about the under-housemaid position." Her voice came out steadier than she'd expected.

The footman nodded and ushered her into an entrance hall that made St Dunstan's Church seem modest by comparison. Marble floors stretched beneath her feet, and a crystal chandelier caught the light from tall windows.

"Wait here," he instructed, disappearing down a corridor.

Moments later, a woman appeared—tall and straight-backed with steel-grey hair and keen eyes that missed nothing. "Miss Whitfield? I am Mrs Marsh, the housekeeper."

Mercy curtseyed as practiced. "Thank you for seeing me, ma'am."

"Father McKinnon speaks highly of you." Mrs Marsh's expression softened slightly. "Come, Lady Elizabeth wishes to meet you as well."

This unexpected news nearly froze Mercy in place. "The mistress herself?"

"Indeed. The Belmonts take a personal interest in those who join their household."

Mrs Marsh led her through corridors lined with paintings to a morning room where sunlight streamed through lace curtains. A woman sat by the window, elegant in a dove-grey dress, while a distinguished gentleman stood nearby.

"Lady Elizabeth, Lord Charles, this is Miss Whitfield," Mrs Marsh announced.

Mercy curtseyed deeper this time, her heart hammering against her ribs.

"Do sit down, Miss Whitfield." Lady Elizabeth's voice was refined but kind. "Father McKinnon tells us you're quite skilled with a needle."

"I learned from my mother, my lady. She was a fine seamstress."

Lord Charles Belmont nodded approvingly. "Good honest work, that. My own business started with my father's single loom, you know."

The conversation flowed more easily than Mercy had dared hope. They asked about her experience, her mother, and the time she'd spent at St Dunstan's. When Lady Elizabeth inquired about samples of her work, Mercy reached into her pocket and produced a handkerchief she'd embroidered with delicate forget-me-nots.

"Why, this is exquisite," Lady Elizabeth marvelled, examining the tiny, even stitches.

"Indeed," Mrs Marsh agreed, impressed. "Such skill would be most useful in the household."

By the time Lord Belmont rang for tea, Mercy's nerves had settled. They spoke not as masters to a servant, but almost as if genuinely interested in her as a person. When Lady Elizabeth mentioned her daughter Constance's upcoming social season and the many gowns that would need attention, Mercy felt a surge of excitement at the prospect of such work.

"Thank you for your time, Miss Whitfield," Lady Elizabeth said, folding the handkerchief and returning it to Mercy with a gentle smile. "Your story and work is truly remarkable."

Lord Belmont nodded in agreement. "We shall need to discuss matters with Mrs Marsh, of course, but I believe we've seen all we need to see."

"We'll send word very soon," Lady Elizabeth added. "Perhaps by tomorrow."

Mercy rose and curtseyed again, her heart fluttering with hope. "Thank you for the opportunity, my lady, my lord."

21

THE JOURNEY HOME

Mrs Marsh escorted her back to the entrance hall, her expression inscrutable. "You carried yourself well," she said, her voice lowered. "Many girls from your circumstances would have been overwhelmed."

"Thank you, Mrs Marsh," Mercy replied, uncertain whether this was praise or merely observation.

The footman appeared at Mrs Marsh's summons. "James will show you out. Lord Belmont has arranged a carriage to return you to St Dunstan's."

Mercy blinked in surprise. "A carriage? For me?"

"Indeed. The Belmonts do not send potential staff walking across London." A hint of approval flickered across Mrs Marsh's stern features. "Good day, Miss Whitfield."

Outside, a gleaming black carriage waited, the Belmont crest emblazoned on its door. The coachman helped Mercy inside, and she sank into plush velvet seats that smelled of beeswax polish and fine leather.

As the horses pulled away from Belgrave Square, Mercy's fingers danced across the butter-soft upholstery. She'd never ridden in such splendour. Through the window, she watched fashionable ladies stroll arm-in-arm, passing shopfronts displaying silks and ribbons that would have made her mother gasp with delight.

The carriage rocked gently as it navigated London's busy streets, moving from the wealthy districts toward the more familiar, crowded lanes of Seven Dials. Mercy's heart raced with each passing minute, possibilities spinning through her mind. Would she soon work in that grand house? Would she sleep in proper servants' quarters with a bed of her own? Would she wear a uniform and be addressed as Miss Whitfield by those below her in the household hierarchy?

The contrast between where she'd been just months ago—feverish and homeless—and where she might soon find herself seemed almost too vast to comprehend. She pressed her hand against the window, feeling the cool glass beneath her finger-tips as Seven Dials came into view, its narrow streets and leaning buildings a stark reminder of all she'd endured.

The carriage drew to a halt outside St Dunstan's. Before Mercy could reach for the door, the coachman opened it and offered his hand.

"Thank you," she murmured, stepping down onto the familiar cobblestones, aware of neighbours watching with undisguised curiosity.

Father McKinnon appeared at the church door, his eyes widening at the sight of the grand carriage.

Mercy hurried inside, cheeks flushed with excitement. Mrs Campbell looked up from her knitting, needles pausing mid-stitch.

"They sent you home in their carriage?" Mrs Campbell exclaimed, as Mercy burst into the vestry.

"Lord Belmont insisted," Mercy explained, sinking into a

chair. "Oh, Mrs Campbell, Father McKinnon—you should have seen the house! It's the grandest place I've ever been."

"And the interview?" Father McKinnon prompted, leaning forward eagerly. "How did they receive you?"

"They were so kind," Mercy said, hands clasped tightly in her lap. "Lady Elizabeth examined my stitching and called it exquisite. Even Mrs Marsh—who looks as though she could freeze water with a glance—seemed to approve."

Mrs Campbell set aside her knitting. "And did they offer you the position?"

"Not yet. They said they needed to discuss it with Mrs Marsh, but would send word very soon—perhaps even tomorrow." Mercy's voice wavered with nervous hope. "Do you think I might actually have a chance?"

"With your talents?" Father McKinnon smiled. "I've no doubt of it."

22

BITTERSWEET FAREWELLS

The letter arrived three days later, delivered by a Belmont footman in smart livery. Mercy's hands trembled as she broke the seal, unfolding crisp paper that bore the Belmont crest.

"They've accepted me," she whispered, her voice catching. "I'm to start next Monday."

Mrs Campbell clapped her hands together. "Praise the Lord! I knew they would see your worth, lass."

Father McKinnon beamed from the doorway. "This calls for celebration. I believe Mrs Campbell has been hiding away some special tea for just such an occasion."

Mercy sank onto a chair the letter pressed against her chest. After months of uncertainty—the bitter cold of London streets, the gnawing hunger, the constant fear—she finally had a place to belong. Secure employment in a respected household. Regular meals. A proper bed.

"Thank you," she whispered, though the Belmonts weren't present to hear. "I won't disappoint you."

The days passed in a flurry of preparation. Mrs Campbell

helped Mercy mend her few garments and offered practical advice about service in grand houses, while Father McKinnon taught her the proper ways to address various members of the household.

On her final morning at St Dunstan's, Mercy took her mother's Bible and placed it carefully into her small bundle of belongings. Beside it lay her most precious possession—her mother's sewing box with its worn wood and brass fittings. She ran her fingers across the lid, tracing the pattern her mother's hands had smoothed over many years.

"Nearly ready, then?" Mrs Campbell appeared in the doorway, her usually brisk manner softened by the occasion.

"Almost." Mercy glanced around the vestry that had become her sanctuary. "I can't quite believe I'm leaving."

Mrs Campbell settled beside her on the narrow cot. From her pocket, she withdrew something small that caught the morning light.

"I have something for you," she said, opening her palm to reveal a silver thimble. "This belonged to my daughter, Fiona. I've kept it all these years, though my own fingers have grown too stiff for fine work."

Mercy stared at the delicate thimble. It was far finer than the simple brass one in her mother's sewing box—its silver polished to a gentle gleam, with tiny engraved flowers circling its crown.

"Mrs Campbell, I couldn't possibly—"

"Hush now." Mrs Campbell took Mercy's hand and pressed the thimble into her palm. "A good seamstress needs proper tools, and this one comes with prayers." Her weathered fingers closed Mercy's around the gift. "Fiona would be pleased to know it's being used by hands as skilled as yours."

Tears welled in Mercy's eyes. "I don't know how to thank you. For everything."

"You already have, lass. Watching you heal and grow these past months has been blessing enough." Mrs Campbell's eyes glistened. "You remind me so much of her—my Fiona. That same quiet strength."

Mercy threw her arms around the older woman's shoulders. Mrs Campbell stiffened momentarily, then melted into the embrace, her hand patting Mercy's back with tender awkwardness.

"You'll do well, Mercy Whitfield. Remember everything you've learned—not just about service, but about faith and endurance."

Father McKinnon appeared in the doorway, his kind face solemn. "The carriage has arrived."

Mercy nodded, wiping her eyes with the back of her hand. She placed the silver thimble in her pocket, nestled beside her mother's brass one.

"Father, I don't know how I'll ever repay your kindness."

He shook his head. "There's nothing to repay. You were a gift to us, Mercy."

"Oi! They sending you off in a fancy carriage again?"

Tommy's voice echoed from the church entrance. He sauntered in, grinning broadly, though his eyes betrayed a hint of sadness.

"Tommy! How did you know I was leaving today?"

"Word travels." He shrugged, hands thrust deep in his pockets. "Couldn't let you go without saying goodbye, could I?"

"I'm glad you came." Mercy took his hand. "Please look after the others. And yourself."

"Always do." He glanced toward the door. "So ... Belgrave Square, eh?"

"It's a good position," Mercy said. "With the Belmonts—a textile merchant's family."

Tommy nodded. "Just don't forget us common folk while you're polishing silver spoons."

"Never," Mercy promised, squeezing his hand. "You can find me there if you ever need help."

Outside, the Belmont carriage waited. Mercy's belongings were loaded by the coachman. She turned for one last look at St Dunstan's, at Father McKinnon's gentle smile, Mrs Campbell's tear-streaked face, and Tommy's casual wave that couldn't quite hide his concern.

As the carriage pulled away, Mercy's hand slipped into her pocket, fingers closing around the silver thimble. The metal warmed against her skin—a tangible reminder of those who had cared for her when she had nothing. The smooth surface against her fingertips felt like a promise, a connection to the past as she journeyed toward her future.

Seven Dials fell away behind her as the carriage rolled toward Belgrave Square and the next chapter of her life.

23
A NEW WORLD

The carriage wheels clattered over cobblestones, each jolt bringing Mercy closer to her new life. She clutched her mother's sewing box tightly against her chest, its familiar weight anchoring her as the vehicle rolled through an ornate iron gateway.

Mercy's breath caught in her throat. The Belmont mansion rose before her, a vision of grandeur unlike anything she had ever seen. Three stories of gleaming Portland stone stood proudly against the spring sky, with rows of tall windows reflecting the afternoon sun. Six white columns framed the entrance, supporting a triangular pediment adorned with intricate carvings.

The carriage came to a halt on the circular gravel drive. Mercy remained frozen in her seat, suddenly aware of her shabby appearance despite Mrs Campbell's efforts with the grey wool dress. How could someone like her belong in such a place?

"Miss Whitfield?" The coachman opened the door, extending his hand.

Mercy swallowed hard and stepped down, her worn boots crunching on the pristine gravel. The gardens surrounding the house stretched in every direction—a sea of green punctuated by bursts of colour from early spring blooms. Carefully trimmed hedges formed intricate patterns, while stone statues gazed serenely from their pedestals.

A fountain played at the centre of the drive, water cascading from the raised hands of a marble maiden. The gentle splashing mingled with birdsong from the surrounding elms and chestnuts, creating a symphony of wealth and privilege that seemed to mock Mercy's humble origins.

The massive oak door swung open before Mercy could reach it. A footman in crisp livery bowed slightly, but before he could speak, a booming voice called from within.

"Ah! Miss Whitfield has arrived!"

Lord Belmont strode through the doorway, his substantial frame filling the space. His dark brown hair, peppered with grey at the temples, framed a face flushed with health and vigour. Deep lines around his eyes spoke of a man who laughed often and heartily.

"Welcome to our home, Miss Whitfield." His handshake was firm but gentle. "I trust your journey was comfortable?"

"Yes, sir. Thank you, sir." Mercy curtseyed as Mrs Campbell had taught her, struggling to keep her voice steady.

"None of that stiffness now." Lord Belmont smiled, the corners of his eyes crinkling. "Father McKinnon speaks most highly of you, and we're delighted to have you join our household."

Mercy relaxed slightly under his approachable manner. The stern-faced Master Belmont she had conjured in her imagination bore little resemblance to this hearty man with kind eyes.

"Charles, do let the poor girl breathe before overwhelming her."

Lady Elizabeth Belmont appeared in the doorway, a vision in pale blue silk. Her dark blonde hair was arranged in an elegant knot, accentuating her oval face and delicate features. She moved with graceful purpose, her skirts rustling softly against the marble floor.

She approached Mercy with a gentle smile, her hazel eyes sweeping over the girl's modest attire.

"My dear, you must be exhausted. We shall see you properly outfitted." Lady Elizabeth nodded approvingly. "A girl with your talents deserves appropriate attire. You'll be part of our family now, in your own way."

The kindness in her voice brought unexpected tears to Mercy's eyes, which she blinked away hastily.

"Thank you, my lady. I'll work hard to deserve your trust."

"I've no doubt you will." Lady Elizabeth smiled. "Now, let me introduce you to our children—or those who are present, at least."

Lord Belmont cleared his throat. "Our eldest, Simon, is away at Oxford. Brilliant mind, that boy. Studying theology, though I'd prefer he showed more interest in the family business." He chuckled, though Mercy detected a hint of genuine disappointment. "Wants to serve in London's poorest parishes rather than pursue the comfortable living I could provide. Noble aspirations, I suppose."

"Charles." Lady Elizabeth placed a gentle hand on her husband's arm. "Simon follows his calling, as we all must."

A young woman descended the sweeping staircase, her light brown hair artfully arranged with ribbons. She moved with practiced grace, chin held high, bright blue eyes assessing Mercy with undisguised curiosity.

"This is our daughter, Constance," Lady Elizabeth said. "She's preparing for her debut in society this season."

Constance offered a perfunctory nod. "Father, is this the new housemaid? The one Father McKinnon recommended?"

"Yes, indeed." Master Belmont beamed. "Miss Whitfield has quite the talent with a needle, which should prove invaluable with all your gowns requiring attention this season."

A flicker of interest crossed Constance's face. "Is that so? Well, we shall see."

From the garden door burst a lanky youth of about thirteen, golden retriever bounding at his heels. His clothes were rumpled, his light brown hair windswept.

"Philip!" Lady Elizabeth admonished. "Where are your manners?"

The boy skidded to a halt, noticing Mercy for the first time. "Oh! Is this the new girl? Hello there!" His grin was infectious, his green eyes alight with mischief.

"Miss Whitfield, this whirlwind is our youngest, Philip," Master Belmont said fondly. "Still at school and running wild whenever possible."

"Not wild, Father. I was conducting an experiment on the velocity of—" Philip caught his mother's stern glance and straightened his posture. "Pleased to make your acquaintance, Miss Whitfield."

"Now, would you like to see the house?" Lady Elizabeth asked Mercy.

What followed was a dizzying tour through rooms more splendid than Mercy had imagined possible. Sunlight streamed through tall windows onto polished mahogany furniture. Thick carpets muffled their footsteps. Oil paintings in gilded frames depicted generations of well-dressed ancestors and pastoral landscapes.

In one room, a massive tapestry depicted a hunting scene

with lifelike hounds pursuing a stag. In another, a pianoforte gleamed beneath a crystal chandelier that scattered rainbows across the walls. The dining room table could have seated twenty, its surface reflecting the silver candelabra positioned along its length.

Mercy struggled to maintain her composure. How many families from Seven Dials could fit into this single house? How many meals could be prepared from what was spent on just one painting?

"It's quite overwhelming at first," Lady Elizabeth said softly, noticing Mercy's expression. "But you'll soon find your place here."

Mercy nodded, praying her new employers couldn't hear the thundering of her heart. This was her chance—her opportunity to build a life beyond survival. Father McKinnon had been right: perhaps this was God's purpose for her after all.

24
THE PATH AHEAD

Lady Elizabeth led Mercy through a small door hidden beneath the grand staircase, revealing the bustling domain of the household staff. The kitchen hummed with activity—a stark contrast to the composed elegance of the upper floors. A large woman with flour-dusted arms barked orders at two scullery maids who scurried between copper pots steaming on the range.

"Cook, this is Miss Whitfield, our new maid," Lady Elizabeth announced.

Cook barely glanced up from her pastry, offering a curt nod. "Another pair of hands won't go amiss. Mind you keep out from underfoot when meals are being prepared."

Mercy bobbed a curtsy, uncertain if she should speak. Before she could decide, a flash of bright red curls caught her attention as a girl about her age burst through the doorway, arms laden with vegetables.

"Betsy, there you are," Lady Elizabeth said. "This is Mercy Whitfield. Perhaps you could show her the servants' quarters once Mrs Marsh has finished with her?"

The girl grinned, revealing a dimple in her left cheek. "Of course, m'lady." She winked at Mercy. "Don't look so frightened. We only eat the new girls who can't sew."

Lady Elizabeth raised an eyebrow, but her lips twitched. "I'll leave you in Mrs Marsh's capable hands now, Mercy."

As if summoned by her name, the tall woman with iron-grey hair pulled into a severe bun strode into the kitchen. Her back was ramrod straight, her dress impeccably pressed. In one hand she held a clipboard, in the other a pencil poised for notation. "Thank you, my lady. I'll take matters from here."

After Lady Elizabeth departed, Mrs Marsh beckoned Mercy to follow her down a narrow corridor to a small office. The walls were lined with ledgers and the desk bore neat stacks of papers.

"So," Mrs Marsh said, settling behind her desk. "Father McKinnon may speak highly of your character and Lady Elizabeth is impressed by your needlework. But running a household like the Belmonts' requires more than moral fibre and neat stitches."

Mercy swallowed hard. "I'm eager to learn, Mrs Marsh."

Something softened in the housekeeper's stern gaze. "Well, that's the right attitude, at least." She tapped her pencil against the clipboard. "I understand you've had a difficult path. Seven Dials is no place for a young girl alone."

"No, ma'am."

"Yet you survived. That shows resourcefulness." Mrs Marsh leaned forward. "And Father McKinnon says you taught those street children to read? Using only a Bible?"

Mercy nodded, surprised this detail had been shared.

"Organisation. Determination. Those are qualities I value." Mrs Marsh stood abruptly. "Your sewing skills will certainly be useful, particularly with Miss Constance's debut approaching, but you'll need to master many other duties."

Over the next hour, Mrs Marsh outlined Mercy's responsibilities: assisting with table settings, tending to the family's linens, helping the kitchen staff during larger gatherings, and naturally, mending and altering garments as needed.

"The household runs like clockwork," Mrs Marsh explained, leading Mercy through the servants' areas. "Each person plays their part. Miss a beat, and the entire rhythm falters."

They paused at the linen cupboard, its shelves stacked with precisely folded sheets and tablecloths. Mrs Marsh ran a finger along one shelf.

"I was fourteen when I entered service. Younger than you are now." Her voice softened with memory. "The housekeeper then, Mrs Fletcher, took me under her wing. Taught me that true skill lies not just in doing tasks well but in anticipating needs before they arise."

She turned to Mercy, her grey eyes intent. "I see something in you, girl. The same hunger I had to rise above my circumstances."

For the first time since arriving, Mercy felt her shoulders relax. "Thank you, Mrs Marsh. I won't disappoint you."

"See that you don't." But the words carried no sting.

The days that followed established a rhythm. Mercy woke before dawn to help prepare the dining room for breakfast. Mornings were spent learning the intricacies of household management from Mrs Marsh. Afternoons often found her mending garments or assisting Betsy, whose cheerful chatter filled even the most mundane tasks with laughter.

"You're catching on quick," Betsy remarked on Mercy's third day as they polished silver together. "Took me weeks to remember which spoon goes where."

"My mother always said attention to detail makes the

difference in sewing. I suppose it's the same with household tasks."

"Your mum taught you well, then. Better than mine, who taught me only to run faster than my brothers when dinner was called." Betsy grinned. "Though I suspect you've stories that would curl my hair tighter than it already is. Seven Dials has a reputation."

Mercy tensed, but Betsy nudged her shoulder gently. "No need to share if you don't want to. We've all got pasts. It's what we do now that matters to Mrs Marsh."

Philip often interrupted their work with boyish enthusiasm, once bringing a frog he'd caught in the garden pond, causing Betsy to shriek and Mercy to laugh despite herself. Even Constance occasionally sought Mercy out, asking her opinion on ribbons for a ballgown or requesting minor repairs to delicate lace.

At night, Mercy returned to her small but private room in the servants' quarters, a luxury beyond imagining after the cellar in Seven Dials. She placed Mrs Campbell's silver thimble beside her bed each evening, a reminder of how far she'd come.

One night, unable to sleep, Mercy slipped to the window overlooking the garden. Moonlight silvered the manicured lawns and cast long shadows from the stone fountains. From somewhere in the house, a clock chimed midnight.

"Thank you," she whispered, unsure if she was addressing her mother, Father McKinnon, or God Himself. For the first time since losing her mother, the path ahead seemed clear. Here, among the Belmonts, she might find not just employment, but purpose.

25
EARLY DAYS

Sunlight streamed through the high kitchen windows as Mercy arranged plates along the worktop with careful precision. Steam rose from the massive copper pot bubbling on the range, filling the kitchen with the earthy aroma of porridge. The clock had barely struck five, yet the kitchen hummed with activity—Cook directing preparations while Betsy darted between tasks, her bright red curls escaping their cap as she worked.

Mercy concentrated on her task, measuring each movement as she'd been taught. Mrs Marsh expected nothing less than perfection, even in the simplest duties.

A sudden burst of laughter jolted her from her thoughts. Betsy stood watching her, wooden spoon in hand, eyes crinkled with amusement.

"Why the long face, dearie? The sun's shining, and we have enough porridge to fill an army!" Betsy's grin widened as she stirred the massive pot. "You look like you're planning a funeral rather than breakfast."

Heat crept into Mercy's cheeks. "I just want to do it properly."

"And you will, but you needn't look so grave about it." Betsy flicked a stray curl from her forehead. "The plates won't run away if you smile at them."

Despite herself, Mercy felt her lips twitch upward. There was something infectious about Betsy's cheer that cut through the morning's solemnity.

"There! A smile! I knew there was one hiding somewhere." Betsy swept past, depositing a pitcher of cream on the tray. "You've been here near a fortnight, and I've scarcely seen you laugh. It's not natural for someone your age to be so serious."

"I suppose I've had little cause for laughter recently."

"All the more reason to find it now." Betsy lowered her voice conspiratorially. "Did you hear about young Master Philip's latest mischief? Put a whole heap of worms in Miss Constance's slipper yesterday morning. Her screams woke half the household—Lord Charles himself came running in his nightshirt!"

Mercy couldn't help but giggle at the image. "Surely not."

"Gospel truth! And last month, he hid behind the curtains during Lady Elizabeth's tea with the vicar's wife and made ghostly noises. Poor woman nearly fainted into her teacup." Betsy's laughter bubbled over as she worked, her hands never stopping their efficient movements.

Throughout the morning, Betsy's stories flowed as steadily as the tea she poured—tales of footmen dropping trays before important guests, Cook's legendary temper when her soufflés fell, and the time Lady Elizabeth's prized lapdog stole an entire pheasant from the dinner table.

Mercy found herself working with a lighter heart, Betsy's cheerful presence making the hours fly past. Even Mrs Marsh's scrutiny seemed less intimidating with Betsy's quiet winks of encouragement.

"You know," Betsy said as they scrubbed vegetables for the midday meal, "the way you study those carrots, I'd think you were searching for Scripture written in the dirt."

"Scripture in vegetables?" Mercy raised an eyebrow.

"Why not? You could find God's hand in a pudding if you looked hard enough." Betsy winked, her freckled face alight with mischief.

Mercy felt a flush of embarrassment, but Betsy's tone held no malice—only friendly teasing.

"My mother always said God speaks through everything if we've ears to hear," Mercy admitted quietly.

"Well, these potatoes are telling me they'd rather not be peeled, but needs must." Betsy nudged Mercy's shoulder gently. "Your faith gives you strength. I admire that, truly. We all need something to hold onto in this world."

The kitchen gradually transformed into Mercy's favourite place in the grand house. Unlike the formal rooms upstairs with their imposing furniture and watchful portraits, the kitchen pulsed with life. Steam clouded windows, pots clattered, knives chopped in rhythm, and through it all ran Betsy's laughter like a bright thread weaving the chaos into something beautiful.

Cook, a formidable woman with forearms like a blacksmith's, maintained order with barked commands that somehow never seemed harsh. Under her reign, the kitchen produced miracles daily—golden pastries, roasts glistening with fat, and confections so delicate they seemed spun from dreams rather than sugar.

"Mind yourself now," Betsy whispered one afternoon as footsteps approached the kitchen. "Margaret Winters is on the prowl."

Mercy glanced up to see a slender woman enter. Though perhaps only a few years older than herself, Margaret Winters carried herself with the authority of someone far more senior. Her dark hair was pulled back severely, accentuating sharp cheekbones and even sharper eyes that missed nothing.

"Cook, Lady Elizabeth requires tea in the drawing room for herself and Miss Constance," Margaret announced, her gaze sweeping across the kitchen before landing on Mercy. "And who might this be?"

"Mercy Whitfield, the new housemaid," Cook replied without looking up from her pastry.

Margaret's lips thinned as she surveyed Mercy from head to toe. "Ah yes, Father McKinnon's charity case. I'd heard Mrs Marsh had taken a fancy to a girl from the streets."

The words sliced through the kitchen's warmth. Mercy felt her shoulders stiffen but kept her eyes lowered, continuing her work.

"Lady Elizabeth speaks highly of your needlework," Margaret continued, her tone suggesting this was somehow suspicious. "Quite the rapid rise for someone so ... recently arrived."

"Miss Whitfield has proven herself capable," Cook interjected, her knife coming down with particular force on the board.

"Naturally." Margaret's smile didn't reach her eyes. "One must wonder, though, what special qualities elevated her so quickly from the gutters to Belgrave Square."

Mercy's hands trembled slightly as she arranged tea cakes on a tray, feeling the weight of Margaret's scrutiny. The kitchen suddenly felt smaller, the air thicker.

"The tea, Miss Winters?" Cook prompted pointedly.

With a final assessing glance at Mercy, Margaret turned

away. "Fifteen minutes, in the blue service." The door swung shut behind her.

Betsy waited until Margaret's footsteps faded before moving to Mercy's side. "Don't let Winters get under your skin; she thinks she's royalty just because she buttons Lady Elizabeth's dresses. Been here since she was twelve and fancies herself mistress of all she surveys."

"She clearly doesn't think I belong here," Mercy whispered.

"Psh! She doesn't think anyone belongs here but herself." Betsy's voice dropped to a conspiratorial murmur. "Just remember, there's plenty of us who know your worth. Mrs Marsh wouldn't have you here if you weren't suited to the position."

Mercy nodded, grateful for the reassurance even as doubt crept in. The grand house with its polished surfaces and gleaming silver suddenly felt alien again, as though she were an impostor who might be discovered at any moment.

But then Betsy bumped her hip playfully against Mercy's, breaking the spell. "Come on then, those cakes won't arrange themselves. And if one happens to break and need eating, well, that's just God's providence, isn't it?"

Despite herself, Mercy laughed, the sound rising to mingle with the kitchen's steam and warmth.

26

BELONGING

Mercy tucked a loose strand of hair behind her ear as she polished the silver alongside Betsy in the servants' hall. Three months had passed since her arrival, and the routines of the Belmont household were becoming familiar —wake before dawn, prepare breakfast, tend to the morning chores, assist with lunch, afternoon duties, evening preparations, and finally collapse into bed, exhausted but satisfied.

"I've never seen spoons so shiny you could see your whole future in them," Betsy remarked, holding up a serving spoon to examine her distorted reflection. "Look at me! I've got the longest nose in all of London in this one."

Mercy couldn't help but smile. "My mother would say that's a sign of good fortune—seeing yourself clearly in silver."

"Was she always full of sayings, your mother?" Betsy asked, her hands never pausing in their rhythmic polishing.

"Always." Mercy's voice softened with fondness. "She had wisdom for everything—weather, cooking, people. Said she learned most of it from my grandmother."

Betsy nudged her gently. "Well, she must've been a

remarkable woman to raise someone like you. I've never seen Mrs Marsh warm to anyone so quickly, and that woman's heart is supposedly carved from London stone."

The compliment warmed Mercy as she focused on a particularly stubborn tarnish spot. These quiet moments with Betsy had become precious—little islands of friendship amidst the sea of work. With each passing day, Mercy found herself standing taller, speaking more confidently, learning to navigate the currents of the great house.

"Polishing silver while gossiping, are we?" Margaret Winters' voice cut through their companionable silence. She stood in the doorway, arms folded across her chest. "Perhaps if you focused more on your tasks and less on chatter, you'd finish before Christmas."

"Nearly done, Miss Winters," Betsy replied cheerfully, seemingly immune to Margaret's barbs.

Margaret's gaze settled on Mercy. "Lady Elizabeth mentioned her lace handkerchief needs mending. I told her I'd attend to it, but she insisted on your 'special touch.'" Her mouth twisted around the words. "One wonders how a girl from Seven Dials acquired such refined skills."

"My mother taught me," Mercy answered softly, continuing her polishing.

"Indeed? And did she teach you that silver requires circular motions, not back and forth as you're doing? You'll leave streak marks." Margaret shook her head. "I suppose we can't expect proper training from the streets."

The silver warmed under Mercy's increasingly vigorous polishing as Margaret departed. She exhaled slowly, willing her cheeks to cool.

"Breathe," Betsy whispered, demonstrating with an exaggerated intake of air. "There you go. Margaret was born with vinegar in her veins instead of blood."

Mercy managed a small laugh. "How do you bear it so easily?"

"Practice," Betsy winked. "And knowing that her misery is her own burden to carry, not mine."

As autumn crept into London, the kitchen transformed into a hive of intensified activity. Preparations for harvest celebrations meant mountains of vegetables to peel, fruits to preserve, and breads to bake. Mercy found unexpected joy in these tasks, especially when working alongside Betsy.

"My dream," Betsy confided one afternoon as they kneaded dough side by side, "is to have my own little bakery someday. Nothing grand, mind you. Just a cozy shop with warm bread and perhaps fancy cakes for special occasions."

"You'd be wonderful at it," Mercy said, pushing her weight into the resistant dough.

"What about you? What's your dream?"

Mercy paused, flour dusting her forearms. "I'd like to have enough—enough to never worry about a roof or food again. And perhaps teach children to read and sew, like I did with the street children."

"Teaching suits you," Betsy nodded, slapping her dough with satisfaction. "You've got patience."

"Not always," Mercy laughed, gesturing at her somewhat lopsided loaf.

"Ah, but bread doesn't judge its shape, only its taste." Betsy shaped her dough with practiced hands. "And neither should we. Your loaf has character—like all the best things in life."

With flour-covered hands and shared laughter, Mercy felt something fragile yet powerful building within her—not just friendship with Betsy, but a sense of belonging she hadn't felt since her mother died.

27
UNEXPECTED KINDNESS

Mercy stood frozen, her heart plummeting to her feet as a crimson splash of ink bloomed across the pale blue silk of Lady Elizabeth's new day dress. The precious bottle had slipped from her fingers when Lady Elizabeth had called for her opinion on the fit. Now disaster spread before her eyes.

"Oh no, I—I'm so sorry, my lady," Mercy stammered, mortification heating her cheeks. Lady Elizabeth's expression shifted from surprise to disappointment.

"Well, that's rather unfortunate," Lady Elizabeth said with a sigh. "I was to wear this to the Burlington's luncheon tomorrow."

Footsteps approached briskly behind them. Margaret Winters appeared in the doorway, taking in the scene with sharp eyes.

"What's happened here?" Margaret asked, moving closer.

"A small accident with the ink," Lady Elizabeth explained, gesturing to the stain.

Mercy braced herself for Margaret's cutting remark, but

instead, the lady's maid stepped forward, examining the fabric with practiced scrutiny.

"Fresh ink on silk? It can be salvaged if we act quickly." Margaret turned to Mercy. "Fetch cold water, salt, and white vinegar from the kitchen. Quickly now."

Mercy blinked in surprise before darting off. When she returned with the supplies, Margaret had already removed the dress from Lady Elizabeth and laid it flat across the table.

"Watch carefully," Margaret instructed, her tone professional rather than condescending. "Cold water first to keep it from setting, then salt to draw it out, followed by vinegar."

Mercy observed Margaret's deft movements as she treated the stain, explaining each step with the authority of someone who'd performed this rescue many times before.

"My mother taught me this trick," Margaret said, almost absently. "She was lady's maid to the Countess of Havershire for thirty years."

"It's working," Mercy marvelled as the stain gradually faded.

Margaret's lips twitched, almost forming a smile. "Of course it's working. Now you'll know for next time, though I trust there won't be a next time."

"No, Miss Winters. Thank you for showing me."

Margaret nodded curtly before turning to Lady Elizabeth. "It will need to dry naturally, my lady. I can prepare the lavender silk as an alternative for tomorrow."

Later that evening, Mercy recounted the incident to Betsy as they prepared vegetables for tomorrow's meals.

"Margaret actually helped you?" Betsy's eyebrows shot up. "Perhaps she's human after all."

"She knew exactly what to do," Mercy said. "It was almost like seeing a different person."

Betsy tapped her knife against the cutting board thoughtfully. "You know, Mercy, you shouldn't hide your light under a bushel either. I've seen your needlework—it's extraordinary."

"It's just what my mother taught me."

"No, it's more than that. You have a gift." Betsy leaned forward, eyes brightening with sudden inspiration. "Lady Elizabeth mentioned the parish charity bazaar next month. What if we created something special for it? You could sew, and I could help with the planning."

"Create what exactly?" Mercy asked, intrigued despite her hesitation.

"Something beautiful. Perhaps a christening gown? Or embroidered handkerchiefs? Things that would showcase your skills and raise good money for the orphanage."

Mercy's fingers itched at the possibility. "Mrs Marsh might not approve of us using our time that way."

"We'd work on it during our free hours," Betsy countered. "And if we tell Mrs Marsh it's for Lady Elizabeth's charity, she might even support the idea."

The seed planted, Mercy found herself warming to the notion. "I could design something with forget-me-nots, like my mother taught me."

"That's the spirit!" Betsy grinned, patting Mercy's hand with flour-dusted fingers.

As the kitchen quieted later that night, only Mercy and Betsy remained, wiping down the last of the surfaces before retiring.

"What do you want, really want, beyond all this?" Betsy asked, gesturing around the kitchen.

Mercy considered the question carefully. "To become accomplished enough that my work is valued for itself, not just as a servant's duty. To perhaps one day have my own small shop, teaching girls to sew properly." She looked up. "What about you?"

"Head cook somewhere smaller than this grand house. Somewhere I could create my own menus, not just follow tradition." Betsy wrung out her cloth. "We're quite the pair of dreamers, aren't we?"

"Dreamers who work hard," Mercy corrected with a smile.

"The best kind." Betsy held out her pinky finger. "Let's make a pact. Whatever happens, we'll help each other reach those dreams."

Mercy linked her pinky with Betsy's. "Like sisters."

"Better than sisters—we chose each other."

Standing at the kitchen window later, needle in hand as she began sketching designs for their charity project, Mercy watched the moonlight silver the garden. From homeless in Seven Dials to here—with friends, purpose, and possibilities stretching before her. The path ahead remained uncertain, but for the first time since her mother's death, Mercy felt truly hopeful. With Betsy's friendship and her own growing confidence, perhaps dreams weren't as distant as they once seemed.

28

A RETURN TO BELGRAVE SQUARE

The morning light had barely touched the grand windows of the Belmont estate when the distinctive crunch of carriage wheels against gravel drew Mercy's attention. She paused in her dusting of the entrance hall sideboard, cloth suspended mid-polish as the sounds of arrival filtered through the heavy oak door.

Footsteps hurried across the marble floor as the butler moved with unusual haste to receive the unexpected visitor. Mercy retreated to a respectful distance, continuing her work while keeping her gaze lowered. The door swung open, allowing a gust of crisp autumn air to sweep into the hall.

"Master Simon! We weren't expecting you until tomorrow."

A deep voice replied, rich with education yet warmly informal. "The college matters concluded earlier than anticipated. I thought I'd surprise everyone."

Mercy glanced up, catching her first glimpse of who she assumed was the eldest Belmont son. Tall and lean, Simon Belmont stood framed in the doorway, his travelling coat dusted with the evidence of a long journey. Dark hair fell slightly across his forehead, giving him a dishevelled appearance that somehow enhanced rather than diminished his natural dignity. But it was his eyes that captured Mercy's attention—deep brown and thoughtful, conveying an intelligence that seemed to take in everything around him in a single glance.

Unlike his father's commanding presence or his sister's self-conscious grace, Simon carried himself with a quiet assurance that suggested comfort with who he was rather than concern for how others perceived him.

As the butler took his coat, Lady Elizabeth's voice rang from the top of the staircase.

"Simon! My darling boy!"

The young man's serious expression transformed with a smile that reached his eyes. "Mother."

Mercy returned to her dusting, moving carefully along the perimeter of the hall as mother and son embraced. Though she kept her eyes on her work, her ears remained attuned to their conversation—not from rudeness but from the natural curiosity that had always been both her blessing and her curse.

"Your father will be delighted. He's in his study going over the quarter's accounts."

"I'll greet him shortly. How is everyone? Constance? Philip?"

"Thriving. Philip's tutor reports marked improvement in his Latin, and Constance has three invitations this week alone."

Their voices faded as they moved toward the morning room, leaving Mercy to complete her task. She had heard much about the eldest Belmont son during her months in service—his academic achievements, his theological studies, and most intriguingly, his unconventional desire to serve in London's poorest parishes rather than accept the comfortable living his father's connections could secure.

The breakfast room buzzed with unusual energy the following morning as Mercy assisted in serving. The family rarely took breakfast together, but Simon's return had drawn them to the table, even Philip, who typically preferred taking toast in his room before lessons.

"Oxford continues to fill your head with impractical notions," Lord Charles said, his tone caught between pride and frustration. "There are perfectly respectable parishes where a man of your education could do good work without subjecting yourself to the filth and disease of Seven Dials or Whitechapel."

Simon passed his cup for Mercy to fill. For the briefest moment, their eyes met—his warm brown gaze acknowledging her presence not as a servant but as a fellow human being—before he returned his attention to his father.

"The filth and disease are precisely why those areas need educated men committed to improvement, Father. Christ didn't minister to the comfortable."

Lady Elizabeth intervened smoothly. "The parish of St Michael's in Kensington has an assistant position opening. Reverend Townshend mentioned it specifically when we last spoke. The vicar there does remarkable charity work."

"From a safe distance," Simon replied without heat. "I've spent time in these neighbourhoods, Mother. Their needs are immediate and desperate."

Mercy moved around the table, keeping her expression neutral despite the subject matter stirring memories of her own life in Seven Dials—the hunger, the cold, Tommy and the children trying to survive each day.

"You've been blessed with advantages, Simon," Lord Charles continued. "Your position in this family creates oppor-

tunities to effect change through proper channels—parlia-
mentary committees, charitable boards. Taking holy orders for
a slum parish wastes those advantages."

Constance leaned forward. "Simon would make a
wonderful politician, Father. He's terribly persuasive when he
wishes to be."

"I have no interest in politics, Constance. My calling is
clear."

The conversation continued in this vein throughout the
meal, with Simon firmly but respectfully maintaining his position against his father's increasingly pragmatic arguments.
Mercy noted how the young man never raised his voice or
showed frustration, yet never wavered in his convictions.

As she cleared away the dishes, Mercy couldn't help but
admire his dedication. His world and hers could not have been
more different, yet something in his determination to help
those society overlooked resonated deeply within her. She
thought of her own dreams—of one day teaching sewing to
children who had no opportunities—and felt a curious kinship
with this young man she had only just met.

Later, as Mercy folded linens in the laundry room, Betsy
burst in with bright eyes and pink cheeks.

"Have you seen him then? Master Simon? Isn't he just as
handsome as everyone said?"

Mercy smiled softly. "He seems very devoted to his beliefs."

"Devoted and dreamy," Betsy sighed dramatically. "Did
you hear him at breakfast? Standing up to his father like that?
Cook says Lord Belmont has been trying to persuade him away
from the church for years."

"It can't be easy to disappoint your father," Mercy replied,
smoothing a pillowcase with careful hands.

"Well, I think it's noble. And so do you—I can see it in your
face."

Mercy didn't confirm or deny this observation. Instead, she changed the subject to their plans for the charity bazaar, but Betsy's words lingered in her mind. Perhaps she did find Simon Belmont's idealism admirable. But admiration was as far as such thoughts could safely go for a girl from Seven Dials working as a housemaid in Belgrave Square.

29
THE FALLEN SPARROW

Simon retreated to the library after breakfast, seeking solace among theological texts rather than continuing the circular argument with his father. The familiar scent of leather bindings and paper calmed his frustration as he settled into the window seat, opening a volume on the early church fathers.

The household's peaceful afternoon shattered when the front door burst open with a bang that echoed through the hallway. Simon looked up from his book to see Philip rush past the library doorway, face flushed and hands cupped protectively against his chest.

"Mother! Father! Come quickly!" Philip's voice carried the unmistakable pitch of urgent excitement.

Simon set aside his book and followed the commotion to the drawing room, where Philip stood before their parents and Constance, carefully opening his cupped hands to reveal a tiny, bedraggled sparrow. The bird's feathers were matted with blood, one wing splayed at an unnatural angle.

"I found him beneath the oak tree in the square," Philip

explained breathlessly. "A cat was stalking him. We must save him!"

Lady Elizabeth stepped back slightly. "Philip, dear, it's very ... commendable that you wish to help, but the creature is clearly beyond saving. And we have the Harringtons arriving for dinner in two hours."

"Your mother's right," Lord Charles added with a dismissive wave. "Nature takes its course, son. Best leave it be."

"We can't just let it die!" Philip protested, his green eyes wide with distress. "Simon, tell them!"

All eyes turned to Simon. He moved closer, examining the tiny creature that trembled in his brother's palms. Its rapid heartbeat was visible through its fragile chest, its dark eye bright with the desperation of a dying thing.

"It does seem badly injured," Simon admitted, his heart tugging at Philip's crestfallen expression. "But perhaps we could try to help it, at least make it comfortable."

"Don't encourage him, Simon," Lord Charles said firmly. "Philip, take that bird outside immediately. Constance needs to prepare for dinner, and your mother has arrangements to oversee."

"Your father's right about the dinner," Simon interjected gently, seeing the determination hardening in Philip's face. "But perhaps one of the servants could help with the bird. Mrs Marsh might know what to do."

Philip brightened momentarily, but Constance scoffed.

"Who among the staff would waste time on a common sparrow?" she asked, adjusting her bracelet. "They all have duties for tonight's dinner."

The conversation ended with Philip reluctantly agreeing to place the bird in a box in the stables, though Simon saw the stubborn set of his brother's jaw that suggested he wouldn't abandon his rescue so easily.

Later that night, after a dinner filled with polite conversation about politics and the upcoming Season, Simon found himself unable to sleep. His thoughts circled between his father's expectations and his own conviction about his calling. As dawn's first light filtered through his window, he decided to walk in the garden to clear his mind.

The kitchen garden lay quiet in the misty morning. As Simon rounded the hedge of rosemary, he stopped short at an unexpected sight. Mercy Whitfield knelt beside the herb bed, focused intently on something in her lap. Her dark hair fell loose around her shoulders, caught by early sunlight in a way that reminded him of stained glass.

Drawing closer, he saw the sparrow from yesterday cradled in a nest of cloth. With remarkable gentleness, Mercy was feeding the creature using a dropper fashioned from a quill. The bird's beak opened eagerly for each careful drop of liquid.

"I didn't expect to find anyone here," Simon said softly, not wanting to startle her.

Mercy looked up, surprise flickering across her face as she recognised him. She made to rise, but Simon gestured for her to remain seated.

"Master Philip was so distressed," she explained, her voice soft but steady. "He brought the bird to the kitchen after everyone retired, begging for help. I couldn't turn him away."

Simon crouched beside her to observe the tiny creature. The sparrow's wing had been bound with a strip of clean cloth, and its feathers, though still damaged, had been carefully cleaned.

"You've tended it all night?"

Mercy shook her head slightly. "Only since dawn, Master Belmont."

"Please, call me Simon."

30
CARE

Mercy felt her cheeks warm at his request. She focused on the sparrow, adjusting its makeshift splint to hide her momentary discomfort. No one of his station had ever asked her to use their Christian name before.

"Why spend so much time on it?" Simon asked, studying her carefully. "It may not survive the day. Even with your care."

The question wasn't cruel, merely curious. Mercy stroked the sparrow's tiny head with her fingertip before answering.

"My mother always said that God notices every sparrow that falls. If He cares enough to notice, shouldn't we care enough to try?" She glanced up, meeting his gaze directly. "Even the smallest creature deserves compassion, doesn't it?"

Simon's expression shifted subtly, his eyes warming with something like recognition. "You sound like someone who's given this considerable thought."

"When we had little else, my mother and I had our faith," Mercy replied, offering the sparrow another droplet of water. "She taught me that our actions matter, however small."

"Even when no one of consequence is watching?" Simon

prompted, settling himself more comfortably on the stone bench beside her.

"Especially then," Mercy said. "That's when it matters most, I think."

The garden grew brighter as they talked, dawn giving way to proper morning. Their conversation flowed with surprising ease—from faith to purpose, from duty to compassion. Mercy found herself speaking freely, forgetting momentarily the vast divide between their stations.

"You've a remarkable understanding," Simon observed, his voice thoughtful. "Were you instructed by your parish priest?"

Mercy shook her head. "Just my mother and her Bible. We read together every evening, no matter how tired or hungry." She smiled at the memory. "Some nights I'd fall asleep to her voice reading Psalms."

"The same comfort I found at Oxford," Simon mused. "Though my professors would be shocked to hear a seamstress from Seven Dials expressing theology with more clarity than many of my classmates."

The sparrow stirred in its nest, attempting to adjust its position. Mercy carefully supported its injured wing.

"We should fashion a proper splint," she suggested. "Something to hold the wing in place while it heals."

Simon rose immediately. "What do you need?"

"Two small twigs, straight and smooth. And perhaps a clean strip of linen?"

He returned moments later with the items, plus a small pot of honey from the kitchen. "Cook uses this for burns and cuts," he explained. "It might help prevent festering."

Together they worked over the tiny creature. Mercy guided Simon's larger hands as he held the sparrow still while she secured the splint. Their fingers occasionally brushed, and each time Mercy felt a curious flutter in her chest that had nothing to do with the bird's rapid heartbeat.

"Master Philip will be delighted," Simon said as they finished. "Where will you keep it?"

"Behind the kitchen stove is warm and quiet. I've made a small box with air holes that should keep it safe."

Simon nodded approvingly. "I'll speak with Mrs Marsh. Ensure you have time each day to tend to our patient."

"Our patient?" Mercy echoed, surprised.

"I'll help," Simon said firmly. "Philip too—he should learn responsibility for the life he's saved." He studied the sparrow, now resting more comfortably in its nest. "Do you think it will survive?"

Mercy considered the tiny creature, its resilience despite overwhelming odds. "With proper care and God's grace, yes. I believe it will."

"Then that's what it shall have," Simon promised, his gaze meeting hers with unexpected warmth. "Care and grace in abundance."

31
MR HATCH

Mercy balanced a silver tray of toast racks and jam pots as she hurried down the narrow back stairs toward the servants' hall. Breakfast for the Belmonts was in full swing upstairs, with Betsy frantically brewing a fresh pot of tea after young Master Philip had accidentally upset the first. The entire household seemed to be moving at double pace this morning, with Lady Elizabeth hosting the Harringtons for luncheon later that day.

"Mind your step there, the floor has just been washed," Mrs Marsh called as Mercy navigated the busy kitchen. Cook was barking orders about the luncheon menu while kitchen maids scurried about with flour-dusted aprons.

Mercy nodded her acknowledgment and slipped past the commotion, making her way to deposit the breakfast remains in the scullery. As she entered the staff dining area, she nearly dropped her tray.

A familiar figure stood by the sideboard, tugging uncomfortably at a stiff collar that seemed to be choking him. The footman's livery looked slightly too large across the shoulders, but there was no mistaking that mischievous profile, those quick, darting eyes that had once spotted constables from fifty paces away.

"Tommy?" The name burst from her lips before she could stop herself.

He turned, and his face lit up with recognition. "Mercy! It's really you!"

She hastily set down her tray and rushed forward, propriety momentarily forgotten. They didn't embrace—that would have been most improper in the servants' hall—but their eyes shone with shared delight.

"What are you doing here?" Mercy asked, looking him up and down in his new livery. "And in footman's clothes, no less!"

Tommy straightened his shoulders, making a comical attempt at the dignity his position required. "It's Thomas Hatch now, if you please," he said with an exaggerated bow that nearly made her laugh aloud. "Footman to the esteemed Belmont household."

"Thomas Hatch," she repeated, testing the name. "It suits you better than Quick-Fingers, I must say."

He grinned, the same street-smart smile she remembered from nights in the warehouse cellar, though his face was cleaner now, his hair neatly combed back. "Not so quick with my fingers these days. Mrs Marsh has eyes like a hawk— caught me flipping a coin between my knuckles yesterday and threatened to have me out on my ear if I showed such 'common habits' in front of the family."

"When did you arrive? I've been here for months now, and never a word about a new footman coming."

"Just yesterday," Tommy replied. "I've been sleeping above the stables until they sort out where to put me. The place is a maze, isn't it? All these rooms and rules and bells ringing at all hours."

Mercy nodded, understanding completely. "The first week, I got lost trying to find the linen cupboard and ended up in Lord Belmont's study. Nearly died of fright when he looked up from his papers."

They shared a quick laugh, the kind that comes from shared experience of a world entirely different from the one they'd known.

"But how did you come to be here?" Mercy asked, glancing nervously over her shoulder. Mrs Marsh could appear at any moment, and idle chatter during working hours was frowned upon.

Tommy lowered his voice. "Father McKinnon. After you got this position, he kept an eye on us—on me and the others. Came around with bread and sometimes a bit of cheese, checking that we were all right." He adjusted his waistcoat, pride evident in his posture despite the ill-fitting uniform. "He said he'd been impressed with how I looked after the younger ones, said I had potential for something better than sweeping crossings all my life."

"Father McKinnon recommended you?" Mercy couldn't hide her surprise.

"Said his last recommendation—you—had worked out so well that the family trusted his judgment." Tommy's grin widened. "Though I expect he didn't mention my former occupation to Lord Belmont. Just said I was a hard-working lad looking for an honest start."

"And the children? Mary and Pip and the others?"

"Still together, mostly. The older ones found odd jobs— Pip's working for a cobbler now, proper apprentice with actual wages. Father McKinnon helped place the little ones with families needing help. Mary's with a milliner's family, learning the trade."

Relief flooded through Mercy. She'd worried about them constantly, especially during the bitter winter months.

"It's not been easy," Tommy admitted, his voice dropping to a whisper. "This place has more rules than the King's court, I reckon."

"You'll learn," Mercy assured him. "I did."

"I knew if you could manage it, I could too," Tommy said. "Though I never thought I'd be wearing someone else's livery and calling grown men 'sir' all day long."

"At least you don't have to empty chamber pots," Mercy whispered with a smirk. "That's the worst of it, I promise."

Tommy's face contorted in horror. "They never mentioned that part."

"Ladies' maids and housemaids only. You're spared that particular delight."

They both jumped as the kitchen door swung open and Mrs Marsh swept in, her sharp gaze immediately finding them huddled in conversation.

"Mr Hatch, I believe you're meant to be polishing the silver for tonight's dinner. And Mercy, those breakfast dishes won't wash themselves."

"Yes, Mrs Marsh," they chorused, exchanging quick glances before hurrying to their duties.

CHAPTER 32 GROWING PAINS

That afternoon, Mercy found Tommy in the pantry, staring in bewilderment at an array of silver serving pieces.

"Which one's for the potatoes?" he muttered, picking up various utensils. "They all look like torture devices."

"That's for serving asparagus," Mercy said, gently taking the tongs from his hands. "This flat one with the scrolled edge is for potatoes."

Tommy sighed. "I don't know how you learned all this. My head's fit to burst with rules."

"You managed to keep six children alive on the streets of Seven Dials," Mercy reminded him. "You're not just quick with your hands anymore; you're quick-witted too. You'll find your footing in no time."

Tommy squared his shoulders. "I hope so. Mrs Marsh caught me bowing like I was diving into the Thames yesterday. Said I looked like a drunken sailor."

"Try bending just from the waist, keeping your back straight," Mercy demonstrated.

"Ah, that's it!" Tommy attempted to mimic her movement but overbalanced, nearly toppling a shelf of crystal glasses.

Mercy stifled a laugh. "Perhaps practice away from breakable items."

At dinner service that evening, disaster struck. Tommy, carrying a water pitcher, approached the table with careful concentration. Mercy watched from her position along the wall, silently willing him to succeed.

Master Philip shifted suddenly in his chair, throwing out an elbow that caught Tommy's arm. Water cascaded across the table, narrowly missing Lady Elizabeth but soaking Lord Belmont's sleeve.

"Blimey—I mean, my profound apologies, sir!" Tommy stammered, reverting to street slang in his panic.

Lord Belmont's face darkened. The dining room fell silent.

"No harm done," came a calm voice. Simon Belmont dabbed at his father's sleeve with a napkin. "Accidents happen to the best of us. I recall knocking over an entire punch bowl at the Harringtons' last Christmas."

The tension broke. Lord Belmont grumbled but allowed himself to be mollified.

Later, in the kitchen, Tommy hung his head. "I'm for it now. Mrs Marsh will have me out before morning."

"She won't," Mercy assured him. "Lord Belmont has already forgotten it. Besides, your quick recovery was quite impressive."

"Was it?" Tommy brightened slightly. "I didn't think 'profound apologies' sounded natural coming from me."

"It's getting there," Mercy laughed.

The household buzzed with preparation for an unexpected visit from Lord Belmont's business associates. Mrs Marsh paced the hall, issuing rapid-fire instructions.

"We need the blue drawing room prepared immediately. Where is Mr Wilson with those fresh flowers? And someone must air out the good linen tablecloth!"

Amidst the chaos, Tommy slipped to Mercy's side. "The guests will be here in twenty minutes, but Wilson's nowhere to be found."

"What about the flowers?" Mercy asked, alarmed.

"Follow me," Tommy grinned, that old street mischief lighting his eyes.

He led her to the garden, nimbly hopping the low wall. "I noticed fresh roses this morning. If we cut them now, arrange them quickly ..."

Ten minutes later, the blue drawing room boasted a magnificent display of freshly cut roses, their perfume filling the air. Mrs Marsh entered, visibly relieved.

"Where did these come from? Wilson said the florist couldn't deliver until tomorrow."

"Mr Hatch's initiative, ma'am," Mercy said. "He remembered the garden roses were blooming."

Mrs Marsh assessed Tommy with newfound appreciation. "Well done, Mr Hatch. Quick thinking indeed."

Tommy's chest swelled with pride.

In the kitchen that evening, Betsy regaled them with imitations of Lady Elizabeth's snobbish cousins while they prepared trays.

"Did you see her face when Cook sent out the pheasant?" Betsy adopted a pinched expression. "'Is this prepared in the French style? I find anything else quite provincial.'"

Tommy doubled over laughing. "Sounds just like old Mrs Finch from Neal Street—always thought her pennies were pounds."

Mercy joined their laughter, feeling a warmth she hadn't experienced since before her mother died—the comfort of belonging among friends.

"How's the sparrow?" Simon's voice interrupted their merriment as he appeared in the doorway. "I thought I might check its progress."

Mercy blushed despite herself. "Healing nicely, sir. It took seed from my hand this morning."

After Simon departed, Tommy waggled his eyebrows suggestively. "The young master seems quite interested in your ... bird-healing abilities."

"Oh, hush," Mercy felt her cheeks burning brighter.

Betsy nudged Mercy playfully. "I've been telling her the same! Young Master Simon never used to visit the kitchens before."

"He's merely concerned about the sparrow," Mercy insisted.

"Yes, the sparrow," Tommy nodded solemnly, then burst into fresh laughter with Betsy.

One afternoon, Mercy overheard two scullery maids whispering in the laundry room.

"She was living in the streets, you know. Father McKinnon's charity case. Margaret says it's not proper, her rising so quickly—"

A shadow fell across the doorway. Tommy lounged against the frame, casually flipping a coin between his knuckles—a forbidden habit he'd seemingly resurrected for this moment.

"Careful with those words," he said lightly, though his eyes had darkened. "Or I might just employ some old street tactics to silence wagging tongues."

The maids scurried away. Tommy winked at Mercy. "Some skills are worth keeping sharp."

"Thank you," she whispered, grateful for his protection.

Late that night, Mercy, Tommy, and Betsy gathered in the servants' hall after the others had gone to bed. Tommy produced three slightly bruised apples from his pocket.

"Courtesy of Cook's rejected basket," he grinned, tossing one to each of them.

"To think," Betsy said, biting into hers, "a few months ago I didn't even know either of you, and now I can't imagine this place without you both."

"I never thought I'd wear shoes without holes," Tommy admitted. "Or sleep in a proper bed every night."

"Do you miss it?" Mercy asked quietly. "The freedom of the streets?"

Tommy considered this. "Sometimes. But not the hunger or the cold." He glanced at both of them. "Not the loneliness either."

"I'd like my own bakery someday," Betsy shared, eyes bright with dreams. "With windows full of cakes and buns."

"I want to be a proper butler," Tommy confessed. "With dignity and respect."

"You?" Mercy teased. "The same boy who used to pick pockets at Covent Garden?"

"People change," Tommy said simply. "You've changed too. Remember how frightened you were that first night in the cellar?"

Mercy nodded. "I thought I'd lost everything. But I was wrong." She looked between her friends. "Sometimes you find family in the strangest places."

Betsy sighed dramatically. "And sometimes you find the young master's eye upon you, Mercy Whitfield!"

"Not that again!" Mercy protested, but her denial held little conviction.

Tommy laughed. "We've come a long way from Seven Dials, haven't we?"

The trio sat in comfortable silence, sharing the simple pleasure of apples and friendship in their new home, far from the streets that had once defined them.

32
THE NEEDLE'S GRACE

Mercy's reputation at the Belmont household grew subtly at first, then unmistakably. It began with Cook asking her to mend a torn lace collar rather than sending it to the seamstress in town. Then Lady Elizabeth's lady's maid sought her help with a loose beading on an evening gown. Soon, even Mrs Marsh deferred to Mercy's judgment on whether a tablecloth was worth salvaging.

"Did you hear?" Betsy whispered one morning as they polished silver together. "Lady Elizabeth told Mrs Finch-Hatton that her new housemaid has 'the touch of an angel with needle and thread.'"

Mercy felt her cheeks warm. "You're making that up."

"I'm not! Tommy heard it himself when he was serving tea." Betsy nudged her playfully. "Even Margaret's stopped her snide remarks since Lady Elizabeth praised your work on her blue silk."

It was true. Margaret had grown noticeably quieter around Mercy since the incident with the torn sleeve. The repair had been so seamless that Lady Elizabeth had called Mercy to her dressing room specially to commend her.

"My mother taught me," Mercy had explained, eyes downcast. "She always said each stitch should be invisible to the eye but present in the heart."

"Your mother taught you exceptionally well," Lady Elizabeth had replied.

Now, as Mercy carried a basket of linens through the main hall, Lady Elizabeth emerged from the morning room with Constance.

"Ah, Mercy. Precisely the person I wished to see." Lady Elizabeth beckoned her closer. "The altar cloths in our chapel are showing considerable wear. I wondered if you might take on the task of creating new ones?"

Mercy's heart quickened. "I would be honoured, my lady."

"Excellent. Mrs Marsh will adjust your duties accordingly." Lady Elizabeth smiled warmly. "I've seen your work. I believe you'll create something truly special."

The Belmont family chapel stood separate from the main house, connected by a short covered walkway. Unlike the grandeur of the mansion, the chapel embraced simplicity—stone walls, modest wooden pews, and tall windows that bathed the small space in gentle light.

Mercy spent hours there, measuring and sketching designs for the altar cloths. The quiet solitude reminded her of evenings with her mother, bent over their shared work by candlelight. She chose a pattern of vines and lilies, symbols of resurrection and purity, working them into a border that would frame the altar.

"This is where you've been hiding."

Mercy startled at Simon's voice. He stood in the doorway, watching her with those thoughtful eyes that always seemed to see more than she intended to reveal.

"I'm creating new altar cloths for your mother," she explained, gesturing to her sketches.

Simon crossed to examine her work. "These are remarkable." His finger traced the pattern of lilies. "My mother will be pleased."

"I hope so." Mercy gathered her courage to ask, "Would you think it presumptuous if I added scripture worked into the border? Just a short verse."

"Not at all. Which verse were you considering?"

"'Consider the lilies of the field,'" Mercy quoted softly. "'They neither toil nor spin, yet Solomon in all his glory was not arrayed like one of these.'"

Simon smiled, a genuine warmth reaching his eyes. "Perfect. I look forward to seeing the finished work."

After he left, Mercy remained in the chapel, her fingers steady as she began the intricate stitchwork that would transform plain linen into something sacred.

Two weeks later, Cook found Mercy in the servants' hall mending one of Philip's shirts.

"There you are, girl." Cook's face beamed with pride beneath her cap. "I've a favour to ask, if you're willing."

Mercy set aside her work. "Of course."

"My daughter's had her first child—a boy." Cook's voice wavered with emotion. "I want to give them a proper christening gown, but my eyes aren't what they used to be for fine work."

"I'd be honoured to help," Mercy replied, genuine warmth filling her voice.

That evening, after her duties were complete, Mercy sat with Cook in the kitchen. The household slept while they worked together on the christening gown, a delicate creation of white cotton and lace.

"My own mother made my children's gowns," Cook reminisced, handing Mercy a spool of thread. "Said a child should enter God's house wearing something made with love."

"My mother taught me that too," Mercy smiled, carefully working tiny flowers along the hem. "She said each stitch carries a prayer."

"Wise woman, your mother." Cook nodded approvingly. "You do her proud with those hands of yours."

They worked in companionable silence broken only by Cook's occasional stories of her own children's christenings. The familiar rhythm of needle through fabric soothed Mercy's soul, connecting her to memories of her mother while building something new in this place that was slowly becoming home.

"It's a gift," Cook said finally, watching Mercy's nimble fingers create a perfect row of satin stitches. "What you have with that needle. A rare gift indeed."

Mercy looked up, surprised by the emotion in the older woman's voice.

"My mother said the same." Mercy paused, needle suspended mid-air. "I never thought it would bring me here, though."

"Life takes us on strange journeys," Cook replied, patting Mercy's hand. "But it seems to me you've found your place among us."

Mercy nodded, unable to speak past the sudden lump in her throat. Instead, she returned to her stitching, each careful movement an affirmation that perhaps, at last, she truly belonged.

33
TRANSFORMATION

The household had settled into its evening rhythms when Constance Belmont burst into the kitchen, her face streaked with tears and her eyes wild with despair. In her arms, she clutched a mass of pale blue silk and lace—her ball gown for the Harrington event, now torn beyond recognition.

"It's ruined!" she sobbed, barely able to catch her breath. "Completely ruined!"

Cook and Betsy exchanged alarmed glances as Constance spread the gown across the kitchen table. A jagged tear ran from the bodice down through the skirt, with smaller rips along the delicate lace overlay. Mercy moved closer, examining the damage.

"The carriage wheel caught it when I was alighting at Lady Spencer's," Constance explained between hiccupping sobs. "Mother will be furious. The ball is only two days away, and everyone who matters will be there!"

Mercy touched the torn silk gently, her mind already calculating stitches and techniques. The damage was severe, but not beyond repair—not for someone with her skills.

"I can fix it," Mercy said quietly.

Constance looked up, her tear-stained face a mixture of hope and disbelief. "You can't possibly. Look at it!"

"I can fix it," Mercy repeated, more firmly this time. "Just trust me."

For a moment, Constance simply stared at her, the young lady's eyes meeting the servants'. Then something shifted in her expression—desperation giving way to the faintest glimmer of hope.

"You're certain?" she whispered.

"Yes, Miss Constance. I promise." Mercy carefully folded the damaged gown over her arm. "I'll need my sewing box from upstairs and perhaps some of the silk threads from Lady Elizabeth's embroidery basket, if you'll permit it."

Constance nodded frantically. "Anything. Take whatever you need. Just ... please make it right."

Once Constance had gone, Betsy eyed the gown with skepticism. "Can you really mend that, Mercy? It looks beyond saving to me."

"It's not just mending it needs," Mercy replied, examining the tears more closely. "It needs transformation."

With Mrs Marsh's reluctant permission, Mercy set up in the small back parlour where the light was best. As the house quieted and midnight approached, her candle burned steadily while her needle flashed in and out of the damaged silk.

What began as desperate repair work soon evolved into artistry. Mercy incorporated the tear into a design, creating a cascade of delicate embroidered flowers that flowed from bodice to hem, strategically placed to disguise the mended sections. Using threads that matched the pale blue precisely, she added touches of silver to catch the light when Constance danced.

Her back ached and her eyes burned, but Mercy worked on.

The gentle rhythm of her needle transported her back to those nights with her mother, when they had worked together to create beauty from simple cloth. She could almost hear Sarah Whitfield's voice: "That's it, love. Let your stitches tell a story."

As dawn's first light crept through the windows, Mercy knotted her final thread and cut it with her small scissors. She stood, stretching her cramped limbs, and held up the gown.

Where there had been ruin, there was now elegance. The tear had vanished, replaced by a meandering path of embroidered forget-me-nots and silver-stitched leaves that seemed to dance across the fabric. The gown was not merely repaired—it was transformed, more beautiful than before.

Mercy carefully laid it across the chaise to await Constance's inspection, knowing she had done more than fix a dress. She had poured her heart into every stitch, creating something worthy of the young lady who, despite their differences in station, needed her help.

34
PRAISE

Mercy had barely managed to freshen up after her night of needlework when the parlour door burst open. Constance stood frozen in the doorway, her mouth forming a perfect O of surprise as she stared at the transformed gown.

"Is that—" Constance approached the chaise with cautious steps, as though the creation might vanish if she moved too quickly. "This cannot possibly be my torn gown."

Mercy remained silent, suddenly unsure if her artistic liberties had overstepped bounds. Perhaps Miss Constance had wanted it precisely as it was before, not reimagined.

Constance lifted the dress with trembling hands, turning it to catch the morning light streaming through the windows. The silver thread glinted among the forget-me-nots, creating the illusion of dew drops on petals.

"It's magical," she whispered. "Better than before. How did you—"

Before Mercy could answer, Lady Elizabeth appeared behind her daughter, curious about the commotion.

"Constance, what's this about your—" Lady Elizabeth

stopped mid-sentence, her eyes widening as she took in the gown. "Heavens above."

"Mercy fixed it, Mother. Look at what she's done!" Constance held up the gown, the cascade of embroidered flowers rippling down the silk.

Within minutes, the small back parlour had become crowded. Lord Belmont arrived, followed by Simon and young Philip. Even Mrs Marsh appeared in the doorway, her usually stern expression softening as she beheld Mercy's handiwork.

"Extraordinary craftsmanship," Lord Belmont declared, adjusting his spectacles to examine the stitchwork more closely. "One would think it was designed this way from the beginning."

Lady Elizabeth approached Mercy, placing a gentle hand on her shoulder. "We are truly fortunate to have you with us, Mercy. This is beyond mere mending—it's artistry of the highest calibre."

Heat rose to Mercy's cheeks as she lowered her eyes. "Thank you, my lady. I only wished to make it right for Miss Constance."

"You've done far more than that," Lady Elizabeth said warmly. "I shall speak with Madame Beaumont about incorporating similar designs into Constance's future gowns."

From the corner of her eye, Mercy spotted Margaret Winters hovering at the parlour entrance. Unlike the others, Margaret's face bore no trace of admiration. Her lips pressed into a thin line, and her eyes—cold as January frost—narrowed as she watched the scene unfold.

"Such fuss over needlework," Margaret muttered just loud enough for the nearby servants to hear. "Anyone would think she'd created the silk itself rather than merely stitching it."

Mrs Marsh shot Margaret a quelling glance before turning

back to Mercy. "You've brought credit to the household staff, Whitfield. Well done."

As the family dispersed, each offering final words of praise, Mercy gathered her sewing implements with hands that still trembled from exhaustion and emotion. Margaret's pointed comments hung in the air like a bad odour, souring the sweetness of the moment.

Later in the kitchen, as Mercy sat with a cup of tea that Cook had insisted she take, Betsy plopped down beside her with characteristic exuberance.

"You should have seen old Winters' face when Mrs Marsh praised you!" Betsy exclaimed, mimicking Margaret's pinched expression to perfection. "Green as garden peas with envy, she was!"

"I heard what she said," Mercy admitted, staring into her teacup.

"Pay no mind to Winters!" Betsy waved dismissively. "You're the best seamstress this house has ever seen. Let her stew!" She nudged Mercy's ribs playfully. "The family knows quality when they see it. That's why they're all singing your praises while Margaret lurks in corners spreading her poison."

Mercy managed a smile. "I don't want to cause trouble, Betsy. I'm just grateful I could help Miss Constance."

"You didn't cause trouble—you solved it!" Betsy insisted. "And in spectacular fashion too. Tommy says even Lord Belmont mentioned your handiwork to his business associates this morning."

Something settled in Mercy's heart then—a quiet resolve that straightened her tired shoulders. Margaret's jealousy was her own burden to bear, not Mercy's. If anything, the woman's bitter comments only highlighted the true value of what Mercy had created.

"My mother always said that beauty speaks for itself,"

Mercy said, setting down her cup with new determination. "Perhaps the best answer to unkindness is simply to create more beauty."

That evening, when her regular duties were complete, Mercy brought out the scraps of silk and lace left from Constance's gown. With deft fingers, she began fashioning a small doll's dress that she would give to Mrs Campbell for the parish charity bazaar. Each stitch was a testament not just to her skill but to her belief that her gift could bring joy beyond the walls of the grand house—perhaps even to children like those she'd once lived among in Seven Dials.

The needle flashed in the lamplight, and Mercy smiled to herself. Let Margaret watch and whisper. Mercy would answer with thread and compassion, creating beauty that spoke louder than any criticism ever could.

35
AN EVENING TO REMEMBER

The Belmont household buzzed with anticipation. Footmen darted through hallways with trays of champagne flutes, while maids gave final touches to flower arrangements. Mrs Marsh's voice rang with authority as she directed the chaos into order, preparing for the arrival of London's finest families.

Upstairs in Constance's chamber, Mercy's hands moved with practiced precision as she fastened the final buttons on the transformed gown.

"Stop fidgeting, Miss Constance," Mercy chided gently, a pin held between her lips. "I can't secure this properly if you keep bouncing about."

"I can't help it!" Constance's eyes sparkled with excitement. "The Martins will be here, and I heard Edward Martin has returned from his Grand Tour." She twisted to examine her reflection, the silver-threaded forget-me-nots catching the light. "Do you think he'll notice me?"

"How could he not?" Mercy stepped back to admire her work. The gown fit perfectly, the embroidery enhancing

Constance's delicate features. "There isn't another dress like this in all of London."

Constance spun once more, the silk whispering against the carpet. "Mother says I have you to thank for that." Her expression softened momentarily. "Truly, Mercy ... thank you."

The genuine gratitude caught Mercy by surprise. For a fleeting moment, the divide between servant and mistress seemed to narrow.

"It was my pleasure, Miss." Mercy retrieved a silver hairpin that had fallen. "Now let's finish your hair before Lady Elizabeth comes looking for you."

A soft knock interrupted them. Simon stood in the doorway, already dressed in formal attire, his dark hair neatly combed back.

"The first carriages are arriving," he announced, then paused, his gaze lingering on his sister. "Constance, you look ... transformed."

"It's all Mercy's doing," Constance replied, smoothing her skirts. "She's worked magic with her needle."

Simon's warm eyes shifted to Mercy. "Indeed she has." A small smile played at his lips. "Perhaps one day you'll grace such an event yourself, Mercy. I should be honoured to stand up with you for a dance."

Heat rushed to Mercy's cheeks. "I'm afraid I don't know the steps, Mr Simon."

"They can be learned," he replied simply, before his father's voice called him from below. "Duty calls. Don't be too long, Constance—Mother wants you to greet the Martins."

After he left, Constance gave Mercy a curious look. "My brother seems quite taken with you."

"I'm sure he's merely being kind," Mercy replied, busying herself with tidying the dressing table.

"Simon is kind to everyone," Constance said, "but he doesn't offer to dance with the kitchen maids."

Before Mercy could respond, Lady Elizabeth appeared at the door, resplendent in emerald silk.

"Constance, darling, you must come down—oh!" Lady Elizabeth's eyes widened. "The gown looks even more beautiful in the evening light. Mercy, you've outdone yourself."

"Thank you, my lady."

"Would you like to see the ballroom before the dancing begins?" Lady Elizabeth asked unexpectedly. "You've contributed so much to this evening's success."

Mercy followed Lady Elizabeth and Constance downstairs, keeping a respectful distance. The ballroom had been transformed—hundreds of candles cast a golden glow over polished floors, while musicians tuned their instruments in the corner.

From her position near the servants' entrance, Mercy watched as guests arrived in their finery. The women's gowns formed a sea of colour—pale blues, rich burgundies, delicate pinks—but none displayed the artistry of Constance's repair.

As the first notes of music filled the air, Mercy spotted Simon leading a young lady onto the dance floor. His earlier words echoed in her mind, but she pushed the thought away. Such dreams were dangerous for a girl from Seven Dials.

Yet standing there, watching the swirl of dancers, Mercy felt a swelling of gratitude. From a freezing doorway on a snowy night to this grand ballroom—her journey had been unlikely at best, impossible at worst. Yet here she stood, her work adorning a society debutante, her skills valued by one of London's finest families.

Whatever challenges still lay ahead, she had come this far through faith and the gifts her mother had nurtured. Perhaps those same gifts would guide her path forward—one careful stitch at a time.

36
A SHARED PURPOSE

W ind rippled through the garden, stirring the leaves as Mercy, Simon, and Philip stood in a circle around the small wicker basket that had served as the sparrow's temporary home. The bird's wing, once limp and bent at an unnatural angle, now looked strong again, the healing complete after weeks of careful attention.

"Do you really think he's ready?" Philip shuffled from foot to foot, his excitement barely contained. He'd visited the sparrow daily, bringing bits of bread and watching with wonder as Mercy changed the splint and cleaned the wing.

"Yes," Mercy answered, keeping her voice gentle. "See how he tests his wing? He wants to be free."

The sparrow indeed seemed restless, hopping about the basket and cocking its head toward the sky. Its recovery had been slow but steady—much like Mercy's own journey from the streets to this place of belonging.

Simon knelt beside his younger brother. "Remember what Mercy taught us about caring for God's creatures. We've done our part, but now we must let him return where he belongs."

Philip nodded solemnly. "Will he remember us?"

"Perhaps," Mercy said, though she doubted it. "But what matters is that we remembered him when he needed help."

Simon lifted the basket closer to Philip. "Would you like to do the honours?"

The boy's green eyes widened. He carefully removed the cloth covering, then tilted the basket. For a moment, the sparrow remained still, seemingly confused by its sudden freedom. Then, with a flutter and chirp, it took to the air, circling once above their heads before disappearing into the oak tree at the garden's edge.

"He's flying!" Philip shouted, jumping up and down. "Mercy, Simon, did you see? He's really flying!"

"Well done, Philip." Simon ruffled his brother's hair. "You've been an excellent physician's assistant."

The boy beamed with pride, then spotted the gardener at the far end of the lawn. "Mr Finnegan said he'd show me the new fountain pump. May I go?"

Simon nodded. "Just don't get your new boots muddy or Mother will have us both scrubbing them."

Philip dashed off, his laughter floating back to them on the breeze. Mercy watched him go, warmth filling her chest at the boy's innocent joy. She began collecting the basket and cloths they'd used for the sparrow's care.

"You've quite a gift with him," Simon observed, helping her gather the items. "Philip can be difficult to engage, but he's hung on your every word these past weeks."

"He has a good heart," Mercy replied. "He simply needed someone to take his concern seriously."

Simon's expression grew thoughtful as they walked slowly along the garden path. "That's what I wanted to speak with you about, actually. Taking concerns seriously." He paused beneath the shade of a chestnut tree, his face earnest. "I hear you grew up in Seven Dials, I have been thinking about that place for a while"

Mercy's hands stilled on the basket. "What about it?"

"I'm starting a small mission there—distributing food and clothing to those in need. Father has grudgingly agreed to support it, though he thinks I'm being foolish." His brown eyes met hers directly. "I could use someone who truly understands the place, Mercy. Someone who knows which families are truly desperate, which children have no one to care for them."

Her heart quickened. "You want me to help?"

"More than help—I need your guidance. I've studied theology at Oxford, but you've lived the realities of Seven Dials. You know the difference between charity that helps and charity that humiliates." He took a breath. "Would you consider assisting me? Mrs Marsh has agreed you could have Sundays free for the work."

Mercy could scarcely believe what she was hearing. The chance to return to Seven Dials not as a beggar but as someone offering help—to perhaps find Tommy's children and ensure they were cared for—it seemed almost too perfect to be true.

"I would be honoured," she said softly. "Truly honoured."

"Excellent!" His face brightened. "I've arranged for a cart of bread and soup this Sunday. We could begin at the crossing near Neal Street."

"The crossing is good," Mercy agreed, her mind already racing with possibilities. "But we should also visit the tenements behind the milliner's shop. There are families there who would never come out to accept charity publicly—their pride is all they have left."

Simon nodded, listening intently. "What else should I know?"

"Blankets would be more welcome than coats as the weather turns," she explained. "A family can share blankets, you see. And perhaps some simple medicines—camphor oil for chest complaints, willow bark for fevers."

"This is exactly why I need you," Simon said, his voice warm with appreciation. "Together, we might make a real difference."

Mercy looked across the grand garden toward the distant rooftops of London, feeling a sense of purpose stronger than any she'd known since losing her mother. To use her knowledge of Seven Dials' hardships to ease others' suffering—it seemed a blessing beyond measure.

"I believe we might," she agreed, her voice steady with newfound determination.

37
THREAD AND NEEDLES

The next morning broke clear and bright over Belgrave Square, a world away from the cramped tenements of Seven Dials. Mercy threaded her needle through a simple linen bag she was fashioning from discarded bedsheets. The servants' hall buzzed with unusual activity as staff prepared for Simon's mission.

"Mind you don't make those too fine," Betsy cautioned, stuffing another bag with dried apples. "Half the families will sell them rather than use them if they look worth anything."

"I never thought of that," Mercy admitted, keeping her stitches deliberately plain.

Simon entered, arms laden with woollen blankets. His shirtsleeves were rolled to the elbows, his collar open—a stark contrast to his usual proper appearance. "These were hidden away in the attic. Mother says they're outdated patterns, but they're perfectly sound."

Tommy appeared behind him, balancing a crate of tinned goods. "Thought these might help. Cook says they've been in the pantry too long for the family's taste."

Mercy watched as Simon directed the growing pile of supplies with the same thoughtful attention he'd given the injured sparrow. Not once did he treat the servants as lesser beings—he worked alongside them, shoulders touching as they sorted and packed.

"You know Seven Dials better than any of us," Simon said, kneeling beside Mercy. "What else do the people there truly need?"

"Thread and needles," she replied without hesitation. "A woman can mend clothing that might otherwise leave her children cold. And soap—it's nearly impossible to stay clean when you can't afford it."

Simon nodded, making notes in a small leather book. "And for the children?"

"Simple medicines," Mercy said, remembering little Mary's fever. "And perhaps a few slates and chalk for those who wish to learn their letters."

By midday, they had assembled more provisions than Mercy could have imagined. The cart stood packed and ready in the mews, a modest miracle of generosity.

38
RETURN TO SEVEN DIALS

Seven Dials looked exactly as Mercy remembered—the crowded buildings leaning into the narrow streets, washing lines strung between windows, the ceaseless noise of too many lives pressed together. Yet something had changed. Not the place, but her place within it.

She walked alongside Simon now, her posture straight, her gaze steady. No longer was she the desperate girl huddled in doorways, clutching her mother's sewing box as her only possession. She returned now with purpose, her skills valued, her knowledge respected.

"We'll start with Mrs. Finch," Mercy said, guiding their small party toward a crumbling tenement. "She has four children and takes in washing despite her hands being near ruined with lye."

Simon's eyes tracked everything—the barefoot children darting between alleys, the hollow-cheeked women, the men whose shoulders bent with the weight of insufficient work. He didn't wear the expression of horrified pity Mercy had seen on charitable ladies' faces. Instead, his gaze held understanding and resolve.

"You've lived this," he said quietly. "I've only read about such conditions."

"But you listened," Mercy replied. "That matters more than you know."

Mrs Finch wept when they presented her with soap, blankets, and food. Her oldest boy, now nearly as tall as Tommy, stood proudly beside her, clearly the man of the family since his father's passing.

"The Lord provides," Mrs Finch whispered, clutching Mercy's hand. "Look at you now, girl. Your mother would burst with pride."

They moved through the tenements methodically, Mercy's knowledge guiding them to families who would never beg but desperately needed help. Tommy knew others from his street days, leading them to hidden corners where children slept rough.

At Neal Street crossing, they distributed bread and soup, creating an impromptu gathering that drew curious onlookers. Simon spoke briefly about St. Dunstan's chapel, inviting any who wished to attend, but made no demands. "The food comes with no requirements," he assured them. "It is given freely, as God's love is given."

Mercy noticed how the street folk responded to his lack of condescension. He spoke to them as equals, listening to their concerns with genuine interest. The theological education at Oxford had clearly taught him more than scripture.

"Mercy! Mercy!" A small voice called out, and Mercy turned to find Mary running toward her, brass button still pinned proudly to her tattered dress. The girl flung herself into Mercy's arms.

"You've grown so much," Mercy marvelled, holding her tight. "And look at you—your cheeks have more colour."

"I'm working for the milliner now," Mary announced proudly. "Just sweeping and fetching, but she says I have clever fingers, like you always told me."

Simon appeared at Mercy's side, smiling as Mary chattered about her new life. When she finally paused for breath, he crouched to her level.

"Would you like to learn more sewing?" he asked. "Mercy here is teaching some of the younger servants at our house. Perhaps you could join them on Thursday afternoons?"

Mary's eyes widened. "Could I really, miss?"

Mercy glanced at Simon, surprised but deeply touched by his suggestion. "Yes," she said firmly. "Yes, I think that would be wonderful."

The afternoon stretched into evening as they emptied the cart of its supplies. When the last blanket had been distributed, Simon and Mercy found themselves sitting on the steps of St Dunstan's, watching the sunset paint the dingy buildings with unexpected glory.

"I understand now," Simon said, breaking their companionable silence. "Why this means so much to you."

"What do you mean?"

"Seeing you today—how you spoke to each person, how you knew exactly what they needed without them having to ask." He turned to face her. "This isn't charity for you. It's justice. Returning something that should never have been taken."

Mercy considered his words. "My mother always said God notices every sparrow that falls. I believe He notices every child without shoes, every mother choosing between heat and food."

"And so should we," Simon agreed. He hesitated, then added softly, "I've never met anyone who understands my calling the way you do, Mercy."

The moment stretched between them, fragile and precious. Mercy felt something shift in her heart—a recognition of how perfectly their beliefs aligned, how easily they worked together, how naturally they understood each other's thoughts.

"We should return before dark," she said at last, though part of her wished to remain in this moment.

Simon helped her to her feet, his hand warm against hers. "Same time next week?" he asked.

Mercy nodded, a smile spreading across her face. "Next week, and the week after that."

They walked back toward Belgrave Square side by side, their shadows stretching long on the cobblestones, occasionally merging into one as they passed beneath gas lamps. The stars emerged above them, distant and bright, like the hope that now burned steadily in Mercy's heart.

39
SHADOWS OF DOUBT

Mercy set fresh linens in the linen press, humming softly as she worked. The past weeks had filled her with purpose—the charity work in Seven Dials, her sewing lessons for the younger servants, and most especially, her conversations with Simon about faith and service. Each interaction left her feeling valued in ways she'd never experienced before.

A soft rustling from the doorway caught her attention. Mercy turned to find Miss Constance standing there, her fine silk dress rustling against the doorframe. The young woman's lips were pressed into a thin line, her bright blue eyes narrowed slightly as she watched Mercy work.

"Is there something you need, Miss Constance?" Mercy asked, dropping into a small curtsy.

"No," Constance replied, her voice cool and measured. "I was merely passing by."

But she didn't move on. Instead, she lingered, fingers tracing patterns on the carved door frame. Through the corridor window behind her, Mercy glimpsed Simon crossing the garden, his tall figure easily recognisable even at a distance.

"My brother speaks highly of your charity work," Constance finally said, a slight edge to her words. "He seems to value your opinions on all manner of things these days."

Mercy felt a flush creep up her neck. "Master Simon is very kind to include me in his mission work."

"Yes. Kind." Constance's gaze flicked toward the window, watching her brother disappear around the corner. "He's always had a soft heart for ... charitable cases."

The words stung, though Mercy kept her expression neutral. She'd noticed Constance watching them lately, had sensed a shift in the young woman's demeanour whenever Simon sought Mercy's company.

"Your embroidery skills are remarkable," Constance continued, fingering the lace at her wrist. "But I wonder if you realise how much attention they've drawn. My debut is still fresh, but suddenly all Mother talks about is your needlework."

Understanding dawned on Mercy. Miss Constance felt overshadowed—by a servant, no less. The thought was so unexpected that Mercy hardly knew how to respond.

From the servants' hall below, voices drifted up—Margaret Winters speaking in hushed but carrying tones: "—quite familiar with the young master, if you ask me. Above her station, certainly."

Another voice murmured agreement, and Mercy's stomach tightened. She hadn't realised her interactions with Simon had become the subject of such scrutiny.

"That's quite enough." Mrs Marsh's commanding voice cut through the gossip like a knife. "Mercy has earned her place in this household through hard work and exceptional skill. I'll not hear another word of such slander."

The voices fell silent. Constance, who'd clearly heard the

exchange as well, gave Mercy a look that mingled triumph and resentment before turning away with a rustle of silk.

Alone once more, Mercy pressed her hands against the cool linen, willing her racing heart to calm. The household was shifting around her, and she suddenly felt as unsteady as she had on the streets of Seven Dials.

40
ANNOUNCEMENT

The bell summoned all servants to attention that afternoon. Mrs Marsh swept through the corridor, her usual stern expression tinged with importance.

"Everyone is needed in the drawing room for an announcement. The family has requested a full household presence."

Mercy exchanged puzzled glances with Betsy as they hurried up the servants' stairs. Through the side entrance, they joined the others lining the walls of the grand drawing room. The Belmonts sat arranged before the fireplace—Lord Charles standing tall with barely contained enthusiasm, Lady Elizabeth perched elegantly beside him, Constance seated primly on a chaise, and Philip fidgeting at the edge of a wingback chair. Only Simon stood apart, framed by the large bay window, his expression unreadable.

"I've gathered you all here," Lord Charles began, addressing both family and staff, "because today marks a significant moment for the Belmont legacy."

His voice carried the weight of announcement; chest puffed with pride. "After much consideration, I'm pleased to share that Simon will be joining me as partner in the textile business, effective immediately."

A collective murmur rippled through the staff. Lady Elizabeth beamed, while Constance clapped her hands together in delight. Only Simon remained still, his shoulders tense beneath his well-tailored coat.

"The arrangements are being finalised," Lord Charles continued. "Simon's education at Oxford has prepared him admirably for commerce, despite his ... other interests." He cast a meaningful glance at his son. "With his intelligence and my experience, Belmont Textiles will reach heights previously unimagined."

Lord Charles raised his glass. "To the future of Belmont Textiles!"

The family echoed the sentiment, Simon's voice noticeably absent. As the staff filed out, Mercy caught Simon's eye. The conflict etched across his features spoke volumes.

Hours later, Mercy knelt in the kitchen garden, harvesting herbs for Cook. The afternoon sun warmed her back as she carefully snipped sprigs of thyme. Footsteps on the gravel path made her look up to find Simon approaching, his cravat loosened and hair slightly dishevelled.

"May I join you?" he asked, his voice rough with tension.

"Of course." Mercy rose and moved to the garden bench, where Simon joined her.

Simon sat heavily, removing his hat and running fingers through his dark hair. "I fear Father has orchestrated quite the trap," he said after a long silence. "He presents this partnership as a gift, but it's his way of keeping me from my calling."

Mercy continued cutting herbs, giving him space to speak freely.

"The business could do tremendous good—fair wages, proper conditions for workers." Simon picked up a fallen leaf, turning it between his fingers. "Father isn't unkind to his employees, but he could do so much more. Perhaps I could influence that."

He sighed deeply. "But every day in those offices is a day I'm not serving in Seven Dials, not ministering to those who truly need help."

"Your father values what he knows," Mercy said softly. "Trade, commerce, social standing—this is his measure of success."

Simon looked at her directly. "What would you do, Mercy?"

The weight of his question hung between them. Mercy set down her shears, considering her words carefully.

"When I lived on the streets, I saw two kinds of charity," she began. "There were those who tossed pennies from carriages, never dirtying their gloves, and those like Father McKinnon who knelt in the mud beside us." She met Simon's gaze. "But there was a third kind too—merchants who offered fair prices and honest work to those society deemed worthless."

She brushed soil from her apron. "Perhaps there's more than one way to serve God's children. The question isn't whether to choose business or ministry, but how to bring ministry into whatever path you walk."

Simon's expression softened. "You've a wisdom beyond your years."

"Not wisdom," she replied. "Just the view from both sides of the garden wall."

The evening light deepened around them, casting long shadows across the herb beds. In the distance, a kitchen maid rang the bell for the servants' dinner.

Their eyes met in the fading light, a moment of shared vulnerability passing between them. Simon's hand remained on her shoulder, his touch gentle yet steady.

"Thank you," he said softly, "for reminding me what truly matters."

The garden fell silent save for the rustling of leaves and distant sounds of the household preparing for evening. Neither moved to break the moment, finding unexpected solace in this shared stillness as dusk gathered around them.

"Winter's coming again," Mercy finally said, her voice catching slightly.

The first hints of Winter crept over the Belmont estate with cold fingers. Mercy pulled her woollen shawl tighter around her shoulders, trying to suppress a shiver.

"The cold never feels quite the same anymore," she admitted quietly. "Not since that winter when I lost Mother. And then nearly myself the following year."

Simon remained silent, his attentiveness urging her to continue.

"The snow fell just like this." Mercy gestured to the first few flakes drifting down. "It's beautiful, truly. But now it reminds me of lying in that doorway at St Dunstan's, feeling warmth when I should have felt cold. That terrifies me still."

She glanced down at her hands, surprised to find them trembling. "The nights are the worst. When darkness falls and the house grows quiet, I remember what it was to be truly alone. To wonder if anyone would notice if I simply ... disappeared."

Simon unwound the scarf from his own neck and draped it gently around hers. The wool carried his warmth, smelling faintly of cedar and parchment.

"I noticed," he said simply. He reached into his pocket and produced a small piece of bread, offering it to her with a tentative smile. "I saved this from lunch. Old habit from Oxford— keeping provisions for late-night studies."

The simple gesture nearly undid her composure. Mercy

accepted it with a nod, unable to speak past the tightness in her throat.

"My father's announcement has left me feeling just as trapped as those bitter nights in my dormitory," Simon confessed. "Different circumstances, but the same sense of walls closing in. Expected to become something that feels like a betrayal of my true self."

"The servants whisper about me," Mercy said. "About us. Margaret ensures I hear it—how I'm reaching above my station, forgetting my place."

"And what is your place, Mercy Whitfield?" Simon asked, his voice low and serious.

"I don't know anymore," she admitted. "I once thought it was clear—to survive, then to serve. But now ..."

"Now?"

"Now I dream of more. Of teaching children in Seven Dials to read and sew. Of creating beauty where there is only struggle." She looked up at him. "What do you dream of, truly?"

"A mission in the poorest parish, where faith meets practical need." His hand found hers on the bench between them. "Fair wages and dignified work for those society overlooks. Books and bread offered with equal measure."

Their fingers intertwined almost of their own accord as they sat beneath the falling snow, two souls finding unexpected sanctuary in shared understanding.

41
REPUTATIONS

Constance Belmont stood at the drawing room window; fingers curled around the velvet curtains as she watched her brother and that girl sitting far too close together in the kitchen garden. Snow dusted their shoulders, yet neither seemed inclined to seek proper shelter. What business had a housemaid sharing private conversations with the son of the house? She'd never known Simon to give his scarf to anyone—certainly not to her when she'd complained of chills.

A cold weight settled in Constance's stomach. Father's announcement about the partnership should have been Simon's crowning moment, the beginning of his proper place in society. Instead, he'd looked trapped, and now sought counsel from a servant girl who couldn't possibly understand their world.

"Miss Constance, would you care for tea?" a footman asked from the doorway.

"No," she snapped, then caught herself. "Thank you."

When the footman departed, Constance returned her attention to the garden. Simon's hand now rested atop

Mercy's. Their heads bent close, sharing secrets like childhood conspirators. The intimacy of it struck Constance like a physical blow.

What did that girl possess that drew everyone to her? First Father McKinnon, then Mrs Marsh, even Constance's own gown had been transformed by those clever fingers into something that outshone every other lady at the ball. The compliments still rang in her ears—not for her beauty or grace, but for the servant's needlework.

Constance's reflection stared back at her from the windowpane, superimposed over the garden scene. The contrast was stark—her with every advantage of birth and breeding, yet somehow lacking whatever essential quality Mercy Whitfield possessed.

The humiliation burned. Had Simon forgotten his position? She'd heard the whispers below stairs, seen the knowing glances between the maids. The household would soon become a nest of gossip if this continued.

Constance straightened her spine and released the curtain. This simply would not do. Simon needed reminding of his responsibilities to the family name, and that girl needed to learn her proper place.

The soft knock at the drawing room door interrupted Constance's thoughts. Margaret Winters entered with practised deference, her starched apron and severe bun embodying the proper order Constance craved.

"Pardon, Miss Constance. I noticed you declined tea and wondered if perhaps you might prefer something else? A hot chocolate, perhaps?"

Constance waved a dismissive hand but didn't send her away. Margaret's presence offered a momentary distraction from the unsettling scene in the garden.

"They're still out there," Constance said, unable to keep the bitterness from her voice. "In the cold, huddled together like—like equals."

Margaret moved closer, adjusting the fire screen with meticulous precision. "Your brother and the housemaid, miss?"

"Mercy Whitfield." The name tasted sour on Constance's tongue. "Father McKinnon's little charity case. She arrived with nothing but that worn sewing box, and now Simon hangs on her every word."

Margaret's lips thinned. "It's not my place to speak on such matters, Miss Constance."

"Oh, do speak freely. I'm quite beyond propriety at the moment."

Margaret folded her hands at her waist, her gaze carefully neutral. "The girl has rather elevated herself quickly. One might wonder what ambitions drive such ... advancement."

"Precisely!" Constance turned from the window, pacing the Aubusson carpet. "It's as if everyone's enchanted by her. Cook praises her, Mrs Marsh defends her, and now Simon ..." Her voice caught. "He's to be Father's partner. There are expectations."

"Indeed, miss. Family reputation must be considered above all."

Constance sank onto the settee, suddenly weary. "I don't understand it, Margaret. What does she possess that I lack? I've had every advantage—education, refinement, position—yet Simon treats her counsel as something precious."

Margaret's expression shifted almost imperceptibly, a calculation passing behind her eyes.

"Perhaps Miss Whitfield's ... background ... appeals to Master Simon's charitable nature. Men often mistake pity for deeper feelings."

Constance looked up sharply. "You think that's all it is? Pity?"

"What else could it be?" Margaret smoothed her apron, a subtle hardness entering her voice. "Though it does invite unfortunate speculation below stairs."

Margaret stepped back, her face settling into professional detachment. "Shall I bring that hot chocolate, miss?"

"Yes. Thank you, Margaret."

As Margaret turned to leave, Constance missed the determined set of the lady's maid's shoulders, the slight tightening of her jaw, the purposeful gleam in her eye. Margaret Winters had made some private decision, but her thoughts remained carefully guarded behind her servant's mask.

42
ACCUSED

The first inkling that something was amiss came during breakfast service. Mercy carried the coffee pot into the breakfast room, where Lord and Lady Belmont sat with Constance. The conversation halted abruptly as she entered. Three pairs of eyes followed her movements, trailing her like ghosts as she poured the steaming liquid with practiced care.

"Will that be all, my lady?" Mercy asked, her voice steady despite the sudden tension prickling her skin.

Lady Elizabeth gave a tight nod. "Yes, thank you, Mercy."

Back in the servants' hall, Betsy's normally bright face was clouded with worry. She tugged Mercy into the scullery, glancing about to ensure they were alone.

"There's trouble brewing upstairs," Betsy whispered. "Lady Elizabeth's emerald necklace has gone missing."

The blood drained from Mercy's face. "Her emerald necklace? The one with the diamond clasp?"

"The very same. Margaret found the jewellery box open this morning—empty as a beggar's pocket."

Mercy's mouth went dry. Just yesterday, she'd been in Lady

Elizabeth's chamber, mending a torn sleeve on her blue walking dress. The jewellery box had sat on the dressing table, closed but not locked.

"They can't think ..." Mercy began, but Betsy's expression confirmed her fears.

"Margaret's been in Mrs Marsh's office this past hour," Betsy said. "And there's talk of constables."

Mercy's hand flew to her throat. "But I never—"

"I know that," Betsy squeezed her arm. "But you were there, weren't you? In her ladyship's room yesterday."

The bell for the drawing room jangled sharply, cutting their conversation short. Mercy moved to answer it, but Mrs Marsh appeared in the doorway, her face grave.

"Not you, Mercy. I'll send someone else." The housekeeper's voice was softer than usual. "Lord Belmont wishes to speak with you in the library. Now."

Mercy's legs turned to water. The short walk to the library stretched like miles, each step carrying her closer to ruin. She thought of the workhouse, of prison ships bound for the colonies. Worse still was the thought of disappointment in the eyes of those who had given her a chance.

"God notices every sparrow that falls," she whispered to herself, her mother's words a lifeline. But for the first time, they brought little comfort.

Lord Charles Belmont stood by the fireplace, one hand resting on the mantelpiece, his expression troubled. Lady Elizabeth sat rigidly in a chair nearby, her face pale.

"Mercy," Lord Belmont began, his voice measured. "I assume you've heard about Lady Elizabeth's necklace."

"Yes, my lord." Her voice emerged as a whisper.

"You were in her ladyship's chamber yesterday afternoon?"

"I was, my lord. Mending the sleeve of her blue walking dress."

Lord Belmont nodded, his internal struggle evident in the tightness around his eyes. "The necklace was discovered missing this morning. It was quite valuable—a family heirloom."

"I understand, sir," Mercy said, fighting to keep her voice steady. "But I never touched the jewellery box, I swear it."

Lady Elizabeth shifted in her chair. "No one wants to believe you would do such a thing, Mercy. Your work has been exemplary." Her voice softened. "But the necklace is gone, and you were there. We must consider all possibilities."

The room swam before Mercy's eyes. After months of building trust, of feeling she belonged, it could all be swept away in an instant. The tenuous acceptance she'd earned now balanced on a knife's edge.

"My lady, I would never—" Mercy's voice broke. "Your family has shown me nothing but kindness. I would rather go hungry on the streets again than betray that trust."

Lord Belmont sighed heavily, rubbing his forehead. "We've ordered a search of the servants' quarters." The regret in his voice was evident. "Including your room, Mercy."

The door opened, and Simon entered, his face tight with concern. "Father, what's happening? I just heard—"

"This doesn't concern you, Simon," Lord Belmont said firmly.

"If it involves accusing Mercy of theft, then it most certainly does concern me." Simon moved to stand beside Mercy, his presence a bulwark against the crushing weight of suspicion.

"Simon, please," Lady Elizabeth began, but he cut her off.

"Mother, you cannot possibly believe Mercy would steal from us. You've seen her character, her dedication."

"What I believe isn't the issue," Lady Elizabeth replied. "The necklace is gone, and we must investigate thoroughly."

"By immediately suspecting the person from Seven Dials?" Simon's voice rose. "That's rather convenient, isn't it?"

Lord Belmont's jaw tightened. "Mind your tone, Simon. This isn't about where Mercy comes from. It's about who had access to your mother's room yesterday."

"And how many others had access?" Simon demanded. "Margaret? The upstairs maids? Constance's lady's maid?"

"We're questioning everyone," Lord Belmont assured him. "But the timing ..." He trailed off, glancing at Mercy with genuine regret.

Mercy felt the walls closing in. The room that had once seemed so grand now felt like a trap. She thought of her mother's sewing box, of the silver thimble from Mrs Campbell, the only treasures she possessed. Would they be taken as evidence of her supposed greed?

"My lord," she said, straightening her shoulders despite her trembling hands. "I give you my word that I did not take the necklace. I have never taken anything that wasn't mine, even when I was starving on the streets."

Simon's hand found her shoulder, a gesture of support that didn't go unnoticed by his parents. "Father, you know Mercy. You've seen her teach the children at St Dunstan's, share what little she has. Does that strike you as the character of a thief?"

"It's not a matter of what I believe," Lord Belmont said, though doubt clouded his eyes. "It's about what I can prove, what I must do to maintain order in this household."

Lady Elizabeth stood, smoothing her skirts. "Perhaps we're being hasty. The necklace might yet turn up."

"And if it doesn't?" Lord Belmont asked. "What then? The Runners? A public accusation?"

The word hung in the air like a blade. Accusation. The thing Mercy had feared since her arrival—that her past would condemn her, that no matter how hard she worked, she would always be seen as the girl from Seven Dials, inherently suspect.

"I'll make my decision by tomorrow morning," Lord Belmont said finally. "Until then, Mercy, you're relieved of your duties."

Simon stepped forward. "Father—"

"That's enough, Simon." Lord Belmont's tone brooked no argument. "My decision stands."

Mercy curtsied, her eyes burning with unshed tears. "Yes, my lord."

As she turned to leave, the disappointment in their eyes cut deeper than any physical wound. The fragile sense of belonging she'd built crumbled like ash. Even if the necklace was found, the shadow of suspicion would linger.

Behind her, she heard Simon's voice, low and determined. "I won't let this stand, Father. Mercy is innocent, and I'll prove it."

The door closed behind her, shutting her out from the family she'd come to love, leaving her alone with the crushing weight of accusation.

43
GOSSIP

Mercy climbed the servants' staircase, each step heavier than the last. The familiar walls of the grand house now seemed to press in upon her, no longer a refuge but a place of judgment. A stolen emerald necklace—and she, with her Seven Dials past, was the natural suspect.

She paused at the landing, steadying herself against the banister. Voices drifted up from below, and instinctively she stilled, not wishing to be seen in her current state.

"Always said there was something not right about that girl." Margaret Winters' cutting tone sliced through the air. "The master's son visiting the kitchens at all hours to see her? Most improper."

"But Miss Mercy's been nothing but—" Betsy's loyal defence was swiftly cut off.

"Nothing but what? Climbing above her station? Getting special treatment?" Margaret's voice dropped to a theatrical whisper that nonetheless carried perfectly. "She was found half-dead in a church doorway, for heaven's sake. And now

Lady Elizabeth's emeralds go missing? I'm not one to say I told you so, but ..."

"You're doing precisely that," Mrs Marsh's firm voice interrupted. "These accusations are premature."

"Are they?" Margaret countered. "Mr Simon defending her so passionately in the library just now? I heard him myself. A proper gentleman doesn't involve himself in servants' matters unless there's something more to it."

"That's quite enough, Miss Winters."

"I'm only saying what everyone's thinking. The girl's been putting on airs since she arrived, with her fancy needlework and her private chats with the young master."

Mercy's cheeks burned. She'd never sought Simon's attention—it had been the sparrow, then the mission work. Nothing improper. Nothing deserving of this whispered venom.

Footsteps approached the stairs, and Mercy hurried upward, unwilling to face any of them. In her tiny room, she closed the door and leaned against it, breathing hard.

Margaret's words would spread like fire through dry kindling. Even if she were proven innocent of the theft, how could she remain here with such poison circulating? The fragile peace she'd found, the sense of purpose, the tentative friendships—all at risk.

Mercy sank onto her narrow bed. She'd survived Seven Dials in winter. She'd endured hunger and sickness and loss. But somehow, the thought of losing her place here, of having everyone believe her a thief and a social climber, cut deeper than any physical hardship.

44
SIMON'S NIGHT

S imon stalked the darkened corridors of the Belmont household, his footsteps muffled by the thick carpets. The grandfather clock in the hall struck two, its solemn chimes echoing through the sleeping house. He'd not found a moment's rest since the accusation against Mercy.

His fists clenched and unclenched as he paced. The library door stood ajar, and he slipped inside, welcoming the familiar scent of leather-bound books and polished wood. Here, at least, he could think without fear of waking the household with his restless movements.

"Ridiculous," he muttered, running a hand through his dishevelled hair. How could anyone believe Mercy capable of theft? The girl who'd nursed a broken sparrow back to health, who taught street children to read from her mother's Bible, who spoke of God's love with such quiet certainty?

The moonlight filtered through the tall windows, casting long shadows across the floor. Simon moved to his father's desk and lit a single lamp, its glow barely illuminating the polished surface. He ought to be preparing for his new role in the family business, yet here he was, consumed by thoughts of a housemaid's reputation.

Not just any housemaid.

Simon slumped into his father's chair, remembering the wounded look in Mercy's eyes when his father had dismissed her. It was the same expression he'd seen on the faces of the poor in Seven Dials—resignation to injustice from those with power over their lives.

"I won't let it happen," he whispered into the empty room. "Not here. Not to her."

His father would say he was being foolish, risking family harmony over a servant girl. His mother would fret about propriety and gossip. Constance would sulk about his divided loyalties. But what good was his Oxford education, his theological training, his position of privilege, if he couldn't protect one innocent person from false accusation?

The memory of Mercy's voice came to him: "My mother always said that God notices every sparrow that falls. If He cares enough to notice, shouldn't we care enough to try?"

45
MERCY'S NIGHT

Mercy sat motionless on the narrow bed, her hands limp in her lap as if they belonged to someone else. The single candle flickered, casting wavering shadows across the whitewashed walls of her small room beneath the eaves. Just hours ago, this space had felt like a sanctuary—the first true home she'd known since her mother died. Now it felt like a prison cell awaiting sentence.

She traced a finger over her mother's wooden sewing box. The smooth, worn surface offered no comfort tonight. Six months of building a life, of earning trust, of believing she might belong somewhere—all crumbling beneath the weight of an accusation she couldn't fight.

A soft knock interrupted her thoughts. The door creaked open to reveal Betsy's copper curls, her usually merry face drawn with concern. Tommy loomed behind her, looking uncharacteristically solemn in his footman's livery.

"We shouldn't be up here," Betsy whispered, slipping inside anyway. "But we couldn't leave you alone."

Tommy closed the door quietly. "It's rot, what they're saying. Pure rot."

Mercy couldn't meet their eyes. "It doesn't matter what's true. Only what they believe."

The bed sagged as Betsy sat beside her, taking Mercy's cold hands between her warm ones. "Mrs Marsh doesn't believe it. She told Margaret off proper when she was running her mouth in the pantry."

"Didn't stop the old crow, though," Tommy added, leaning against the doorframe, arms crossed. "Poison, that one."

A tear slipped down Mercy's cheek. "I thought ... I thought I'd finally found a place where my past didn't matter. Where people saw me, not just where I came from."

"They do," Betsy insisted. "Lady Elizabeth was beside herself when Cook told her you'd been crying. Said she hated to think you felt they'd judged you already."

Tommy straightened. "Young Master Simon's been prowling about like a caged tiger. Nearly bit James's head off when he made some comment about street folk. And I heard him telling his father that questioning you was an insult to Father McKinnon's judgment."

The mention of Simon sent a fresh wave of pain through Mercy's chest. She'd seen the anger in his eyes when he burst into the library, but beneath it had been something that frightened her more—a fierce protectiveness she couldn't allow herself to name.

"It's worse, somehow," Mercy said quietly. "Being defended. Like I'm still the girl from Seven Dials who needs saving." She stared at her hands, calloused from years of needlework. "I don't want their pity."

"It's not pity," Tommy said firmly. "Simon respects you. We all do."

Betsy squeezed her hands. "We know you didn't take that necklace. And we'll stand by you, whatever happens."

Mercy looked at her friends—Betsy with her kind heart, Tommy with his streetwise loyalty—and felt the first crack in her wall of despair.

"I can't lose this," she whispered. "Not after everything. This house, this life ... you two ..." Her voice caught. "I've nowhere else to go."

"You're not going anywhere," Tommy said with surprising fierceness. "I've seen things disappear in grand houses before. Truth has a way of coming out."

Betsy nodded. "And till it does, we're here."

Mercy wanted to believe them, but the cold fear in her stomach wouldn't relent. The Belmonts had given her everything—purpose, safety, respect. One missing emerald necklace was all it took to remind her how fragile her position truly was, how quickly she could fall from grace back to the streets that nearly claimed her life.

"Thank you," she said softly, "for risking Mrs Marsh's wrath to come up here."

"What are friends for?" Betsy smiled, though her eyes remained troubled. "Try to sleep. Tomorrow will sort itself out."

But as they slipped away, Mercy knew sleep would not come. Tomorrow loomed before her like a gathering storm, and all she could do was wait for it to break.

46
CONFRONTATION

Simon paced outside his father's study the next morning, rehearsing arguments that seemed to dissolve in the face of his mounting frustration. The household stirred to life around him, but he'd barely slept, spending the night puzzling through possibilities and potential solutions. How could his father so readily believe Mercy capable of theft?

When the clock in the hall struck eight, Simon knocked firmly on the study door.

"Come." His father's voice carried the weight of authority Simon had known all his life.

Lord Belmont sat behind his mahogany desk, already dressed impeccably, his morning correspondence arranged in neat piles before him. He glanced up, his expression hardening upon seeing Simon.

"I've already made my decision about the girl."

Simon remained standing, hands clasped behind his back. "Her name is Mercy, Father. And I implore you to reconsider."

"There's nothing to reconsider." His father's pen scratched across paper, the sound harsh in the quiet room. "The necklace went missing after she was in your mother's chambers. The evidence—"

"Evidence?" Simon stepped forward. "What evidence? That she was born in Seven Dials? That she once lived on the streets through no fault of her own?"

Lord Belmont set down his pen with deliberate care. "Mind your tone, Simon."

"I apologise for my tone, but not for my conviction." Simon took a steadying breath. "You've always taught us about justice and fairness. Where is the fairness in condemning Mercy without proof?"

His father's jaw tightened. "I've been in business long enough to recognise patterns. People rarely change their nature."

"But that's precisely it—Mercy's nature is honest to the core." Simon leaned forward, palms flat on the desk. "Did you not notice how she built literacy classes for the servants? How she tends to Philip when he's upset? How she works twice as hard as anyone else to prove her worth?"

Lord Belmont rose from his chair, his patience visibly fraying. "What I notice, son, is your unusual interest in a housemaid. An interest that has the entire household gossiping."

Heat crawled up Simon's neck. "This isn't about me. It's about justice."

"Is it?" His father circled the desk, his voice dropping dangerously. "The Belmont name means something in this city. Our reputation—"

"Our reputation should be for fairness, not prejudice," Simon interrupted. "You didn't see her face when you accused her. She looked ..." He hesitated, remembering the wounded dignity in Mercy's eyes. "She looked betrayed. As if the trust she'd placed in this family had been thrown back at her."

His father's expression darkened. "I won't be lectured

about trust by my own son. Not when you've been sneaking about with this girl, undermining my authority."

"I haven't been 'sneaking about'!" Simon struggled to keep his voice even. "I've been working with Mercy on the Seven Dials mission, nothing more."

"And the garden conversations?" Lord Belmont shook his head. "The servants see everything, Simon."

Simon straightened his shoulders. "Then you should know that everything they've seen has been above reproach. I admire Mercy's character, her faith, her resilience—qualities you'd appreciate if you weren't so determined to see the worst in her."

"Enough!" Lord Belmont slammed his palm against the desk. "My decision stands. The girl will be dismissed by noon."

"Father, please. I'm asking you to trust my judgment. I know Mercy is innocent."

Lord Belmont regarded his son with a mixture of frustration and disappointment. "And I'm telling you that your judgment is clouded by sentiment. This discussion is finished."

Simon opened his mouth to argue further, but the resolute set of his father's shoulders told him it would be futile. For now.

47
DISMISSAL

Mercy stood alone in her attic room, folding the few dresses she owned with trembling hands. The grey wool dress Mrs Campbell had altered for her interview seemed a lifetime ago. She packed them carefully in the small carpet bag Tommy had found for her, alongside her mother's Bible. Only her sewing box remained on the bed, its familiar worn edges a reminder of everything she had lost before and was losing again.

A sharp knock interrupted her thoughts.

"Miss Whitfield." It was the first footman, Wilson. "Your presence is required in the drawing room. Immediately."

Mercy's heart stuttered. She had expected to be dismissed without ceremony, slipping away through the servants' entrance with only her shame as company.

"All of them are waiting," Wilson added, his usual pompous manner softened slightly. "The entire family."

The long walk down the servants' staircase felt like a funeral march. Whispers followed her, some sympathetic, others vindicated. Margaret Winters stood at the bottom of the stairs, arms folded across her chest, her thin lips curved in the ghost of a smile.

"Good luck, dear." Her voice dripped with false sweetness. "Perhaps the workhouse will take you in."

Mercy lifted her chin and walked past without acknowledgment. She wouldn't give Margaret the satisfaction of seeing her crumble.

The Belmont family waited in rigid formation in the drawing room—Lord Charles standing before the fireplace, Lady Elizabeth perched on the edge of a chair, Constance beside her mother, and Philip fidgeting uncomfortably on a footstool. Simon stood apart from them, tension radiating from his tall frame. His eyes met hers as she entered, filled with fury and helplessness.

"Miss Whitfield." Lord Belmont's voice cut through the silence. "I've called you here to inform you formally of your dismissal from this household."

Mercy clasped her hands to stop them trembling. "Yes, sir."

"The evidence against you is—"

"There is no evidence!" Simon stepped forward. "Father, you cannot do this. It's unjust and beneath our family's principles."

Lord Belmont's face hardened. "Simon, we've discussed this matter exhaustively."

"No, we haven't." Simon's voice rose. "We've dismissed Mercy's character without consideration. What of her service to this household? Her tireless work with the poor of Seven Dials? Her teaching the younger servants to read?"

"Simon, please." Lady Elizabeth's voice wavered. "This is difficult enough—"

"It's not difficult, Mother—it's wrong!" Simon turned to face his family. "We claim to be Christians, to believe in charity and fairness, yet at the first test of those principles, we abandon them entirely."

Constance rose from her chair. "Simon, you're being ridiculous. The necklace is worth hundreds of pounds, and she—" She gestured dismissively toward Mercy. "She was in Mother's chambers just before it disappeared."

"As were you, Constance," Simon retorted. "As was Margaret Winters. As was every maid who turned down the bed or delivered laundry."

"That's enough!" Lord Belmont's voice thundered through the room. "My decision is final. Miss Whitfield will leave this house immediately. Without a character reference."

The last words fell like stones. Without a reference, no respectable household would hire her. Mercy felt the ground shifting beneath her feet, the careful future she had built crumbling to dust.

"This is monstrous." Simon's voice dropped dangerously low. "You condemn her to poverty and hardship without proof of wrongdoing."

"Simon!" His father's face purpled with rage. "You will not question my authority in this house!"

Mercy found her voice at last. "Please, sir." She addressed Lord Belmont directly. "I understand your decision, though I maintain my innocence. I am grateful for the opportunity this household has provided me, however brief."

Her quiet dignity seemed to unsettle Lord Belmont more than Simon's fury.

"You may collect your belongings and leave within the hour," he said stiffly.

Simon stepped toward Mercy, his eyes burning with a mixture of rage and determination. "This isn't over. I'll find the truth, I swear it."

"Simon, don't." Mercy shook her head slightly. Making

more trouble would only damage his position in the family further.

"I won't stand by while an innocent person is condemned." He turned back to his father. "What would you have said to the men at Oxford who dismissed my ideas without consideration? You taught me to fight for what I believe in."

"I taught you to respect this family and its name!" Lord Belmont slammed his hand against the mantelpiece.

"The Belmont name means nothing if it doesn't stand for justice." Simon's words hung in the air, an irretrievable challenge.

Philip suddenly scrambled to his feet. "Mercy didn't take it! She wouldn't! She saved that sparrow when nobody else would."

"Philip, be quiet." Lady Elizabeth tugged at her youngest son's sleeve.

"No!" Philip stomped his foot. "It's not fair! Mercy's good, and you're being horrible to her!"

Mercy felt tears welling in her eyes at the boy's defence. "Thank you, Master Philip," she whispered.

Lord Belmont pointed toward the door. "You are dismissed, Miss Whitfield."

With a final curtsy that cost her every ounce of strength, Mercy turned and left the drawing room. She could hear Simon's voice rising again behind her, but she couldn't bear to listen. Her chest felt crushed beneath the weight of injustice and heartbreak.

Back in her room, Mercy finished packing her meagre possessions. She placed her mother's sewing box carefully on top, running her fingers across its worn surface.

A soft knock preceded Betsy's tear-streaked face appearing at the door. "It's not right," she choked out, rushing to embrace Mercy. "Everyone knows you'd never steal."

"Not everyone," Mercy said quietly.

Tommy appeared behind Betsy, his face tight with controlled fury. "Let me talk to Lord Belmont. I know things about Margaret—"

"No, Tommy." Mercy gripped his arm. "You've built a life here. Don't throw it away on my account."

Mrs Marsh arrived last, her normally stern face softened with concern. "This is poorly done," she said quietly. "I've told His Lordship as much."

"Thank you, Mrs Marsh." Mercy straightened her shoulders. "For everything you've taught me."

"This isn't finished, girl." Mrs Marsh pressed something into Mercy's hand—a small purse that jingled with coins. "To tide you over."

"I can't—"

"You can and you will." Mrs Marsh's tone brooked no argument. "Father McKinnon will take you in, I'm sure of it."

The final walk through the servants' hall was a blur of sympathetic faces and whispered good wishes. At the back door, Mercy turned to Betsy and Tommy one last time.

"Take care of each other," she managed.

Tommy's hands clenched into fists. "I should go with you—"

"No." Betsy and Mrs Marsh spoke in unison, each grabbing one of Tommy's arms.

"She's right," Mercy said softly. "Making more trouble won't help anyone."

She stepped out into the winter air, her breath clouding before her. The chill bit through her thin coat as she walked down the mews toward the street, carpet bag in one hand, sewing box tucked under her arm. Tears blurred her vision, but she refused to let them fall. Not here. Not yet.

At the gate, she paused and looked back at the grand house

that had briefly been her home. In an upper window, she caught a glimpse of Simon watching her, his hand pressed against the glass. The distance between them seemed insurmountable now—not just in station but in circumstance.

Mercy turned away and stepped onto the street, into a future as uncertain as the grey London sky above.

48
WANDERING

The snow came down in angry swirls, stinging Mercy's cheeks as she trudged through the foreign streets away from Belgrave Square. Each step felt heavier than the last, her carpet bag growing more burdensome with every corner turned. The wind knifed through her wool coat—a fine garment by Seven Dials standards, but woefully inadequate against this bitter January cold.

Mercy had forgotten how the buildings here seemed to lean inward, as if conspiring to block what little light filtered through London's perpetual grey. The narrow passages between tenements funnelled the wind into vicious gusts that snatched at her shawl and tore at her carefully pinned hair.

Three hours ago, she had been Mercy Whitfield, trusted housemaid to the Belmont family. Now she was again just a girl from the streets, with nowhere to lay her head.

"Watch yerself, miss!" A cart rattled past, splashing dirty slush onto her skirt. The driver didn't look back.

Mercy pressed herself against a grimy wall, momentarily shielded from the wind. Father McKinnon would take her in—

Mrs Marsh had been right about that. But pride kept her feet moving in the opposite direction from St Dunstan's. How could she face him, bearing the stain of accusation? How could she explain that all his efforts to place her in a respectable household had ended with her dismissed as a thief?

"Not yet," she whispered, her breath visible in the frigid air. "I need time."

Her fingers, numb despite her gloves, clutched her mother's sewing box tighter. The emerald necklace worth hundreds of pounds ... as if she would risk everything for trinkets. As if all those months of building trust and proving herself could be forgotten over mere jewels.

A group of finely dressed gentlemen passed, not sparing her a glance. Just weeks ago, she had served such men tea in the Belmont drawing room. They had smiled politely, thanking the invisible maid who poured so precisely. Now she was truly invisible, another shabby figure haunting London's meaner streets.

Margaret's smug expression flashed in her mind. "I've been saying all along that girl couldn't be trusted," she had heard through the door. The memory burned hotter than any fire. Had Margaret planned this? Or merely seized the opportunity when it arose?

The wind changed direction, driving snow directly into Mercy's face. She turned down a side street, recognising with a start the shabby doorway where she and Tommy had once sheltered during a summer thunderstorm. Tommy, who had survived by his wits and quick fingers. Tommy, who now wore livery and poured wine for lords. Tommy, whose eyes had flashed with fury at her dismissal.

"God helps those who help themselves," she murmured, recalling one of her mother's favourite sayings. But what help was there for a dismissed servant without references?

The snow thickened, blanketing the cobblestones and muffling the street sounds. Mercy passed the milliner's shop where Mary now worked, its windows dark and shuttered against the weather. Should she knock? Ask for shelter? The thought withered as quickly as it formed. Mary's position was as precarious as Tommy's had been. She couldn't risk bringing trouble to the girl's door.

As the afternoon light faded to evening gloom, Mercy's legs trembled with cold and exhaustion. She had walked for hours, retracing old pathways through Seven Dials, postponing the inevitable decision of where to spend the night. The weight of the day's events pressed upon her shoulders, heavier than any physical burden.

"I tried so hard," she whispered to no one. "I did everything right."

A memory surfaced—Simon teaching Philip how to play chess in the library, the firelight catching in his dark hair as he explained each piece's purpose with infinite patience. Mercy had paused while dusting, watching their easy camaraderie, feeling a warmth that had nothing to do with the crackling fire.

Another memory—Betsy's laughter in the kitchen as they kneaded bread, flour dusting their aprons. The comfort of Mrs Marsh's rare smile when Mercy mastered a particularly difficult household task. Little Philip's delight when the sparrow took flight from his outstretched hands.

Gone. All gone.

The snow was falling more heavily now, the flakes fat and wet against her face, clinging to her eyelashes and melting into tears she refused to shed. Mercy ducked into a narrow alley between a tavern and a shuttered shop, seeking momentary respite from the relentless weather.

She leaned against the cold brick wall, sliding down until she sat upon her carpet bag. Her mother's sewing box rested in her lap, the last tangible connection to a life that made sense. Mercy wrapped her arms around herself, trying to preserve what little warmth remained in her body.

The sounds of the city—cart wheels creaking, distant voices calling, the ever-present rumble of commerce—seemed to recede, leaving her in a pocket of silence broken only by her own ragged breathing. In this moment of stillness, the full weight of her situation descended like the snow accumulating on her shoulders.

"I don't know what to do," she admitted to the empty alley, her voice small against the vastness of her circumstances. "I don't know where to go."

49
THE SEARCH

S imon paced the length of his bedroom, unable to settle. The howling winter wind rattled the window panes, each gust a reminder that Mercy was somewhere out there, alone and without shelter. He'd argued with his father until his voice grew hoarse, but Lord Belmont remained unmoved, his face a mask of aristocratic indifference.

"I cannot do this ..." Simon muttered, grabbing his heaviest coat from the wardrobe. He could no longer sit idle while injustice prevailed.

He slipped down the servants' staircase, avoiding the main hallway where his parents might spot him. The back corridors were quiet save for distant clattering from the kitchen. Simon paused at the narrow door that led to the male servants' quarters, knocking softly.

Tommy appeared almost instantly, as if he'd been waiting.

"Young master," he said, his voice formal despite the concern etched across his features.

"I need your help," Simon said simply.

Tommy nodded, already reaching for his coat. "I've been wondering how long it would take you to come knocking."

They slipped out through the mews, the stables providing cover from curious eyes. Fat snowflakes fell relentlessly from the darkening sky, rapidly covering their footprints.

"She's not at St Dunstan's," Simon said as they trudged through the thickening snow. "I sent a boy with a message, and Father McKinnon replied she hasn't sought shelter there."

Tommy frowned, pulling his cap lower against the biting wind. "She's got too much pride for her own good. Always did."

"Where would she go? You know her better than anyone."

"Seven Dials, most like," Tommy replied, his breath clouding before him. "It's what she knows. But it's a labyrinth if you don't know your way around."

"Then we're fortunate I have you with me."

They pushed forward into the heart of London, the elegant streets of Belgrave Square giving way to increasingly narrow, crowded thoroughfares. Simon's fine boots were soon soaked through; his toes numb with cold. He thought of Mercy, whose shoes were thin and worn—how much worse her suffering must be.

As they entered Seven Dials, Tommy transformed before Simon's eyes. The careful, proper footman disappeared, replaced by a street-wise youth who moved with confident familiarity through the warren of alleys and passageways. He nodded to shadowy figures huddled in doorways, exchanged quiet words with a one-eyed man selling matches, slipped a penny to a hollow-cheeked child.

"Gathering intelligence," Tommy explained, catching Simon's questioning glance. "These streets have a thousand eyes. Someone will have seen her."

An hour passed with no sign of Mercy. Simon's worry

deepened with each empty doorway and vacant alley they checked. The snow fell heavier now, obscuring visibility and muffling the usual street sounds.

"She could be anywhere," Simon said, unable to keep the desperation from his voice.

Tommy stopped abruptly, grabbing Simon's arm. "Wait. The boy back there—he mentioned a girl with a wooden box who passed the milliner's shop earlier."

"Her mother's sewing box," Simon breathed. "Which way?"

They doubled back, following the child's directions toward a row of shabby shops with darkened windows. The snow swirled around them in blinding eddies as they pressed forward.

"There!" Tommy pointed suddenly, his keen eyes catching what Simon had missed—a small figure huddled in a narrow passage between buildings.

Simon's heart leapt to his throat. He pushed through the snow-thick air, calling out as he approached the alley.

"Mercy!"

She looked up, her face pale as the snow around her, eyes wide with shock. For a moment, she seemed unable to comprehend his presence, as if he were a vision conjured by her exhausted mind.

"Simon?" Her voice was barely audible, cracked with cold.

He knelt before her, heedless of the wet snow soaking through his trousers. Her lips were blue-tinged, her body trembling violently beneath her inadequate coat.

"We've been searching everywhere for you," he said, removing his scarf and wrapping it gently around her neck. The wool still carried his body's warmth.

Tommy appeared beside them, his face tight with concern. "You're half-frozen, you daft girl. What were you thinking, not going to Father McKinnon's?"

"I couldn't—" She broke off, a violent shiver running through her. "I couldn't bear his disappointment."

"There's no disappointment," Simon said firmly, taking her ice-cold hands between his warm ones. "Only concern for your safety."

Tommy crouched down, examining her critically. "She needs warmth, and quick. The cold's gone deep."

Simon nodded, already helping Mercy to her feet. She swayed dangerously; her legs unsteady beneath her.

"I've got you," he murmured, supporting her weight against him. "I won't let you fall."

50
FOUND

Mercy stared up at Simon, his face blurred through her exhaustion. The snow had soaked through her dress, numbing her limbs until she could scarcely feel them. His arms around her were solid, real—the only warmth in a world gone cold and hostile.

"Why are you here?" she asked, her voice threadbare and weak. The question held all her confusion—why would the son of a wealthy merchant trudge through a snowstorm for a dismissed servant? Why would he risk his father's wrath?

Simon's eyes, dark and serious in the fading light, held hers. "Did you think we would abandon you? That I would?"

Tommy snorted, brushing snow from her shoulders with rough affection. "Told the young master we'd find you. Knew you wouldn't go far—too sensible, even when you're being foolish."

"I'm disgraced," Mercy whispered, the words catching in her throat. "A thief in the eyes of your family."

"Not in mine," Simon said firmly. He knelt beside her, his

warmth radiating through the bitter cold. "Listen to me, Mercy. You're innocent, and I intend to prove it. We couldn't leave you out here. You should be with us—there's a way to clear your name."

Her body trembled uncontrollably, though whether from cold or emotion she couldn't tell. "How? Lord Belmont has made his judgment."

"My father sees what he expects to see," Simon replied, jaw tightening. "But Tommy has been telling me about Margaret Winters. Something doesn't sit right."

Tommy nodded vigorously, his eyes gleaming with street-smart determination.

Hope flickered briefly in Mercy's chest, then guttered out. "Even if you found something, who would believe a street boy and a housemaid over Lady Elizabeth's personal maid?"

"Evidence speaks louder than station," Simon said. "But first, we need to get you warm and safe."

"Father McKinnon and Mrs Campbell will take you in," Tommy added. "We've already sent word ahead."

"You really think they'll let me stay?" Mercy whispered, vulnerability etching her words. "After everything?"

Simon's expression softened. "Mrs Campbell's already warming soup and preparing your bed. Father McKinnon never doubted you for a moment."

Tears sprang to Mercy's eyes, thawing something frozen inside her. "I was afraid to face them—to see disappointment where once there was only kindness."

"There's no disappointment waiting," Simon assured her, helping her to her feet. "Only open arms."

Tommy grinned, shouldering her carpet bag. "And Mrs Campbell's fresh bread, if we're lucky."

Mercy managed a faint smile at that. Tommy's familiar teasing felt like a balm against the sharp edges of her fear.

"Can you walk?" Simon asked, his hand steady at her elbow.

"I think so," she replied, though her legs trembled beneath her.

"Lean on me when you need to," he said simply.

They made their way slowly through the thickening snow, Tommy leading the way through shortcuts and narrow passages. Despite the bitter cold, Mercy felt warmer with each step, wrapped in Simon's scarf and flanked by her loyal friends.

"Betsy sends her love," Tommy reported as they walked. "Says she's keeping an eye on that Margaret for us. And Mrs Marsh—you should have seen her face when Lord Belmont announced your dismissal. Looked like she'd bitten into a lemon, she did."

"She defended you," Simon added. "Said it was premature to judge without evidence."

These small kindnesses, these threads of connection, strengthened Mercy's resolve. Perhaps she hadn't lost everything after all.

51

WELCOMING DOORS

T he wooden doors of St Dunstan's Church creaked open, welcoming Mercy like an old friend. Heat from the fireplace rushed out to meet them, embracing her frozen limbs in blessed warmth. The sudden contrast from bitter cold to gentle warmth made her skin tingle painfully as sensation returned. Inside, dozens of candles flickered across the altar and along the walls, casting dancing shadows that softened the stone edges of the sanctuary.

Mercy paused at the threshold, suddenly hesitant. The church represented safety, yet a small part of her feared to cross that boundary—as though accepting help meant accepting failure.

"Come," Simon murmured, his hand at the small of her back offering gentle encouragement. "You're half-frozen."

The familiar scent of beeswax candles and old prayer books filled her nostrils, carrying memories of the months she'd spent healing here after her collapse. How strange that she should return under similar circumstances—cast out, vulnerable, in need of sanctuary.

Father McKinnon stood at the altar, arranging hymnals, when he heard their footsteps echo across the flagstones. He turned, his weathered face lighting with relief.

"Mercy," he said, his Irish lilt warming her name as he hurried down the aisle. "Thank the Lord you're safe."

She braced herself for disappointment or recrimination, but found only genuine concern in his deep brown eyes. Without hesitation, he enfolded her in a gentle embrace, his cassock rough against her cheek.

"You are safe here, my dear. We will work through this," he said simply, the words carrying the weight of a promise.

"I've brought trouble to your doorstep again," Mercy whispered.

Father McKinnon released her with a soft laugh. "Trouble finds its own way in this parish. You've brought nothing but your good heart."

Tommy stamped snow from his boots. "Smells like Mrs Campbell's been cooking."

"Indeed she has," Father McKinnon nodded. "And praying for Mercy's return since Master Simon sent word."

As if summoned by her name, Mrs Campbell appeared in the doorway leading to the vestry, flour dusting her apron and a wooden spoon clutched in her hand like a sceptre. For a moment, she simply stared at Mercy, her lined face a picture of maternal concern. Then she bustled forward, clucking her tongue.

"Look at ye, child. Soaked through and pale as milk." Her Scottish burr was thicker with emotion. "Come by the fire before ye catch your death."

The vestry had been transformed in Mercy's absence. A pot of soup bubbled on the hearth, filling the air with the rich aroma of beef and vegetables. Freshly baked bread sat cooling on the table, its golden crust promising comfort.

Mrs Campbell took Mercy's frozen hands between her warm, floury ones. "Ye'll be wanting dry clothes first, then food in your belly."

"I don't deserve such kindness," Mercy said, her voice catching.

"Pish," Mrs Campbell scoffed. "Ye deserve that and more. Now sit while I fetch ye something warm."

Later, dressed in a borrowed nightgown and wrapped in a woollen blanket, Mercy sat at the kitchen table with a bowl of steaming soup before her. Simon and Tommy recounted their search while Father McKinnon listened intently, his expression thoughtful. Mrs Campbell bustled about, pressing second helpings upon everyone with fierce determination.

The candlelight cast a golden glow across their faces— Simon's resolute profile, Tommy's animated gestures, Father McKinnon's gentle eyes, Mrs Campbell's nurturing presence. These people believed in her without question.

A small flame of hope kindled in Mercy's chest, warming her from within. Whatever tomorrow might bring, she would face it surrounded by those who truly saw her—not as the girl from Seven Dials, but as Mercy Whitfield, worthy of love and justice.

52
INVESTIGATION

Simon sat alone in the family chapel's front pew, the silence pressing against his ears. A single candle flickered on the altar, illuminating the embroidered cloth Mercy had lovingly created. His theological texts lay forgotten in his quarters—this was a different kind of study, one where souls and livelihoods hung in the balance.

He spread a sheet of paper across his knees, pen poised as he sketched a timeline. Mother's emerald necklace had gone missing Tuesday afternoon. Lady Elizabeth had worn it Sunday evening for dinner with the Harringtons, returned it to her jewellery box Monday morning, and discovered it missing when preparing for the Thornfield reception.

Who had access to Mother's chamber during those critical hours? The list grew quickly: Margaret as lady's maid, Mercy for the mending, Betsy delivering fresh linens, housemaids during morning cleaning, even Constance might have entered.

His pen tapped against the paper. Something nagged at him—not just the injustice of Mercy's dismissal, but the convenient timing. Why now, when Mercy had gained the household's trust? Why the emerald necklace, visible enough to be quickly missed?

THE SERVANTS' hall hummed with activity as Simon approached. Conversation halted abruptly, uncomfortable glances darting his way before everyone returned to their tasks with exaggerated focus.

"Master Simon," Mrs Marsh acknowledged with a respectful nod. "Was there something you needed?"

"Just stretching my legs," he replied casually. "Father's business associates have monopolised the drawing room with talk of cotton prices."

His casual tone had the desired effect. Shoulders relaxed, and the normal rhythm of kitchen work resumed. Simon lingered, asking innocuous questions about dinner preparations and household schedules.

"The timing of Mother's necklace going missing was unfortunate," he remarked to no one in particular. "Right before the Thornfield reception."

Cook shook her head. "Terrible business. Never had thieving in this house before."

"Did anyone notice anything unusual that day?" Simon asked, keeping his tone conversational. "Any strangers about, or disruptions to the normal routine?"

A kitchen maid piped up. "Only thing different was Miss Winters coming down for more polish than usual. Said Lady Elizabeth wanted everything extra shiny for the Thornfields."

"Twice she came," another added. "Morning and afternoon both."

Simon nodded thoughtfully, filing away the information as he continued his casual interrogation.

"I DIDN'T nick things like that," Tommy explained as they sat in the stable loft that evening. "Too risky, too easy to trace. Small items from market stalls, purses from distracted shoppers—that was more my way before."

"But if someone wanted to steal a necklace?" Simon pressed.

Tommy's fingers danced in demonstration. "Quick hands are only part of it. You need to know when and where. Inside job like this—they'd need to know Lady Elizabeth's routines, when the necklace would be unwatched."

"Margaret would know that," Simon mused.

"And timing matters," Tommy continued. "If I wanted to blame someone, I'd make sure they were in the room that day. Make sure others saw them there."

Simon recalled how Margaret had sent Mercy to Lady Elizabeth's chamber for additional mending—work that could have waited another day.

"What if someone didn't just want the necklace?" Simon asked slowly. "What if they wanted Mercy gone?"

Tommy's expression hardened. "Then they'd make sure she took the blame. Plant evidence, spread gossip, point fingers before anyone else could think straight."

Exactly what Margaret had done.

THE FOLLOWING MORNING, Simon requested breakfast in his room, positioning himself near the window overlooking the servants' entrance. He watched each staff member depart for their half-day, noting Margaret's unusually fine appearance as she stepped out.

"Where does Margaret go on her afternoons off?" Simon asked Betsy later, helping her carry linens as pretence for conversation.

"Whitechapel, usually," Betsy replied. "Says she visits her cousin, but Mary from the kitchen followed her once—curiosity, you know—and said she went into some pawnbroker's shop instead."

The pieces began fitting together. Simon sought Tommy immediately.

"Whitechapel pawnbrokers," he said urgently. "Could they fence jewellery?"

Tommy's eyebrows rose. "Certain ones, yes. They'd break it down—emeralds sold separate from the setting."

"How long would that take?"

"Days, maybe. If the stones are large, they might wait longer. Harder to sell without questions."

Simon nodded, mind racing. "Margaret's been spending beyond her means. New shawl last month, those tooled leather shoes, and Cook mentioned a silver hair comb."

Tommy whistled softly. "Either she's got a wealthy admirer, or ..."

"Or she's been stealing small items and selling them," Simon finished. "But Mother's emerald necklace would be worth more than all those combined."

"And worth sacrificing Mercy to get away with it," Tommy added grimly.

Simon stared out the window, jaw tightening with determination. "We need to catch her in the act. And I think I know how."

53
A PLAN

Simon paced the length of his small study, his boots wearing a path in the carpet as Tommy outlined his suggestion.

"I've kept certain connections from my days in Seven Dials," Tommy explained, leaning forward in his chair. "Fellows who know the right people in Whitechapel. If I put out word that there's a gentleman interested in acquiring special items—no questions asked—I might learn what Margaret's been up to."

Simon halted mid-stride. "You're suggesting we pose as potential buyers?"

"Not we," Tommy clarified, a shadow of his street confidence returning to his posture. "Me. Or rather, a version of me nobody at the house would recognise." He smoothed his footman's jacket self-consciously. "I'd need different clothes, of course. But I know how to talk like I belong in those circles."

"It's dangerous," Simon objected. "If Margaret discovers you ..."

Tommy's laugh carried the hard edge of his former life.

"She wouldn't know me if I stood beside her. Mr Hatch the footman bears little resemblance to the sort who frequents Whitechapel pawnshops."

Simon studied Tommy's face, seeing both the polished servant and the street-wise boy beneath. The transformation Tommy had achieved at the Belmont household sometimes made Simon forget his origins—and his skills.

"This isn't merely about clearing Mercy's name anymore," Simon said quietly. "If Margaret has been systematically stealing from my family, we need proof."

"And we need to know where Mother's necklace is," he added, more to himself than Tommy.

Tommy leaned back, crossing his arms. "If she's sold it already, we might never recover it. But if she's waiting for the commotion to die down ..."

"Then it might still be in her possession," Simon finished, excitement building. "What do you need?"

"Clothes that suggest money but not refinement. And a story about a wealthy merchant seeking unique jewellery for his mistress." Tommy's eyes gleamed with the challenge. "My old mate Barney keeps ears open in Whitechapel. He'll spread word that I'm looking to buy."

Simon nodded. "And if Margaret approaches your 'character'?"

"Then I express interest in emeralds. Specifically, ones that might have come from a particular necklace." Tommy's grin turned wolfish. "If she's got it hidden away somewhere, the prospect of a generous buyer might make her careless."

"How long will this take?"

"Give me three days to establish the character. Then another two to let word circulate." Tommy straightened his shoulders. "Market day in Whitechapel would be best. Crowds provide cover."

Simon pulled out his pocket watch, calculating. "That's cutting it close. Father expects me to sign the partnership papers next week."

"Better move quickly then," Tommy replied.

The next afternoon, Simon handed Tommy a bundle of clothes—not his own fine garments, but ones purchased from a second-hand shop in Covent Garden. They showed quality without being ostentatious, perfect for Tommy's merchant character.

"My contact says Margaret visits a particular tavern after the pawnshop," Tommy reported, examining the clothes with approval. "The Twisted Anchor. Barney's already spreading rumours about a gentleman seeking special merchandise."

"Be careful," Simon warned. "If she suspects anything—"

"She won't," Tommy assured him, his voice carrying the hard confidence of Seven Dials. "I learned deception before I learned proper grammar."

Two days later, Tommy returned with news that made Simon's pulse quicken.

"It's arranged. Margaret took the bait—Barney says she approached him asking about the buyer interested in emeralds." Tommy's eyes shone with triumph. "We meet at The Twisted Anchor on Thursday."

Simon clasped Tommy's shoulder. "Well done."

"We haven't caught her yet," Tommy cautioned, but his voice betrayed his excitement.

"No," Simon agreed, "but the trap is set."

54
EXPOSED

The Twisted Anchor reeked of stale beer and unwashed bodies. Simon crouched in the shadows across the street, pulling his borrowed hat lower to shield his face. He barely recognised Tommy in the merchant's garb—a waistcoat of faded burgundy beneath a practical brown coat, hair slicked back with pomade, and a swagger that suggested money earned through questionable means.

Tommy disappeared into the tavern at precisely eight o'clock. Simon's hand moved to his waistcoat pocket, fingers brushing the cool metal of his father's pocket watch. Twenty minutes. That's all Tommy had requested before Simon was to follow.

Across the street, a woman in a dark cloak hurried toward the tavern, her familiar gait causing Simon's pulse to quicken. Margaret Winters. He shrank deeper into the shadows as she passed, noting the fine wool of her cloak—too fine for a lady's maid, unless she had other sources of income.

The minutes crawled by. Simon's breath fogged in the cold air as he waited, watching drunken sailors and painted women pass by. When twenty minutes had elapsed, he straightened his plain coat and crossed the street.

The tavern's interior was thick with pipe smoke and conversation. Simon slipped through the crowd toward the back corner where Tommy sat opposite Margaret, their heads bent close in conversation. A half-empty bottle stood between them. Simon settled at a neighbouring table, angling his body away while straining to hear.

"—quality that would impress even royalty," Margaret was saying, her voice carrying a silky confidence Simon had never heard in the servants' hall. "The craftsmanship alone makes it worth twice my asking price."

Tommy chuckled, the sound nothing like his usual laugh. "Pretty words, Miss Winters. But I deal in certainties, not promises. My client doesn't part with coin without seeing the merchandise."

"And risk you taking my supplier to cut me out?" Margaret scoffed, taking a sip from her glass. "I wasn't born yesterday."

"Nor was I," Tommy countered, leaning back with calculated indifference. "Plenty of others offering similar wares. Just last week, a footman from Mayfair brought me silver candlesticks that—"

"Trinkets," Margaret interrupted with disdain. "What I'm offering is a once-in-a-lifetime opportunity." She lowered her voice, forcing Simon to strain his ears. "Three perfect emeralds, larger than a man's thumbnail, set in gold with diamonds between. The centre stone alone would buy you a house in Bloomsbury."

Simon's heart hammered against his ribs. Mother's necklace.

Tommy maintained his façade of casual interest, swirling amber liquid in his glass. "Sounds like something that might be missed. Recent acquisition, is it?"

Margaret's laugh held a cruel edge. "Let's just say its former owner believes some little guttersnipe made off with it. Convenient, really—the girl had been getting above herself."

The glass in Simon's hand nearly shattered in his grip.

"You arranged for someone else to take the blame?" Tommy asked, sounding impressed rather than appalled.

"Easiest part of the whole affair," Margaret boasted, clearly warming to her audience. "The master's son had been making eyes at her—disgusting business. But men are fools for a pretty face, even one from the streets." She leaned forward. "So, are you interested? I've other buyers circling."

Tommy drained his glass. "I'd need to see it first."

"Of course," Margaret nodded. "I don't keep such valuables on my person. But for a serious buyer ..." She hesitated, then made her decision. "I have a room nearby. It's there, along with other pieces that might interest your client."

Simon watched them leave, counting to fifty before following at a distance.

Margaret led Tommy to a narrow house three streets away. Simon waited in a shadowed doorway opposite, watching Tommy signal with a quick adjustment of his hat—their prearranged sign that Simon should wait five minutes, then follow.

The minutes passed like hours. Finally, Simon crossed the street and climbed the worn steps to the second-floor room Tommy had indicated.

Inside, he found Tommy holding Margaret firmly by the arm while she struggled, her face contorted with fury.

"You lying snake!" she spat at Tommy. "You're that street friend from the house!"

Tommy merely tightened his grip. "Look under the mattress," he told Simon. "Left corner."

Simon lifted the thin mattress and found a cloth-wrapped

bundle. Inside lay his mother's emerald necklace, its stones catching the dim lamplight. Beneath it were several smaller pieces he recognised from the house—silver salt cellars, a pearl brooch that had belonged to his grandmother, and a gold pocket watch his father had reported missing months ago.

"It seems we've found a pattern of theft," Simon said, his voice dangerously quiet. "And evidence of who truly took my mother's necklace."

Margaret's struggles ceased, her face draining of colour. "You can't prove anything," she whispered. "It's my word against yours—a lady's maid against a street thief."

"Evidence speaks louder than either," Simon replied, gathering the stolen items. "As does your own boasting in the tavern."

"What happens now?" Tommy asked, still maintaining his grip on Margaret.

Simon straightened, tucking the necklace into his pocket. "Now we return to Belgrave Square. I believe my father will be most interested in what we've discovered." His gaze hardened as he looked at Margaret. "And in clearing Mercy's name."

55
RETURN

Mercy stood at the grand entrance of the Belmont mansion, her fingers clutching her mother's sewing box. The Portland stone façade loomed above her, imposing and majestic as ever, yet somehow different now. Three days ago, she had left this place in disgrace, accused of theft, her character stained. Now she returned, vindicated but wounded.

Simon stood beside her, his hand hovering near her elbow without quite touching it. "Are you ready?" he asked, his voice gentle.

"I don't know," Mercy admitted, her eyes fixed on the heavy oak door. "It feels as though I'm entering a stranger's home."

"It's still the same house."

"But I'm not the same person who left it."

The door swung open before Simon could respond. Wilson, the butler, stood in the entrance, his face a careful mask of professionalism. If he was surprised to see Mercy, only the slightest twitch of his eyebrow betrayed it.

"Master Simon," he acknowledged with a slight bow. "Miss Whitfield. Lord Belmont is expecting you in the library."

The grand entrance hall felt endless as Mercy walked across the polished marble floor. Every portrait on the wall seemed to watch her with judging eyes, every ornament a witness to her humiliation. The Persian carpet beneath her feet was the same rich blue and crimson she had cleaned a hundred times, yet today it felt like walking across burning coals.

Lord Belmont stood by the fireplace when they entered, his face drawn with uncharacteristic weariness. Lady Elizabeth sat nearby, her fingers restlessly twisting her handkerchief.

"Miss Whitfield," Lord Belmont said, stepping forward. The usual authority in his voice had softened to something approaching contrition. "I owe you an apology. A grave injustice was done to you in this house."

Mercy stood straighter, finding strength in the truth of her innocence. "Yes, my lord. It was."

A flicker of surprise crossed his face at her directness, followed by something that might have been respect.

"My son has explained everything. Margaret Winters has confessed to the theft of the emerald necklace and numerous other items. She has been taken into custody." Lord Belmont cleared his throat. "I was hasty in my judgment and wrong to dismiss you without proper evidence. The position is yours again, should you wish to return."

Mercy felt Simon's eyes on her, but kept her gaze level with Lord Belmont's. "Thank you, my lord. I would like time to consider your offer."

Lady Elizabeth rose from her chair, coming to stand beside her husband. "We would be most grateful if you returned, Mercy. The household has not been the same without you."

Mercy's throat tightened at the sincerity in Lady Elizabeth's voice. She managed a small curtsy. "Thank you, my lady. That's kind of you to say."

After a few more minutes of awkward conversation, Simon escorted Mercy from the library. "You don't have to decide immediately," he said as they walked down the corridor. "Father understands you need time."

"Does he?" Mercy asked. "Or does he simply want his household back in order with minimum fuss?"

Simon's steps faltered. "That's unfair."

"Is it?" She sighed, softening her tone. "Forgive me. I find I'm not quite ready to be gracious yet."

"You've earned the right to feel whatever you're feeling," Simon said, leading her toward the servants' staircase. "Would you like to see Betsy and the others?"

Mercy nodded, squaring her shoulders as they descended into the domain she had once considered home.

The kitchen fell silent as Mercy entered. Betsy stood by the range, wooden spoon frozen mid-stir. Cook's hands stilled over a half-rolled pastry. Two scullery maids—the same ones who had gossiped about her days before—shrank back against the sink.

"Mercy!" Betsy broke the silence, rushing forward to embrace her. "I knew you'd be back. I told everyone, didn't I?" She turned to the others. "Didn't I say they'd sort it all out?"

Cook nodded, wiping her hands on her apron before approaching. "It's good to see you, girl. Place hasn't been right without you."

The warmth of their welcome loosened something in Mercy's chest, yet she couldn't help noticing the scullery maids exchanging glances, or how Wilson stood stiffly by the door, his expression unreadable. The kitchen felt divided—those genuinely glad to see her, and those merely accepting her return because they must.

Mrs Marsh appeared at the doorway, her stern face softening at the sight of Mercy. "There you are," she said briskly.
"When you've finished your hellos, I'd like a word in my sitting
room."

An hour later, Mercy climbed the narrow stairs to her attic
room. Everything had been cleared out. Mercy wasn't sure if it
had been stored or destroyed, but she didn't really have the
mind to worry about that right now. She had her sewing box,
that's what mattered. Someone had dusted and aired the
space, perhaps Mrs Marsh herself.

Mercy set her sewing box on the little table and sank onto
the bed. The silence wrapped around her like a shroud. Here,
alone, she finally allowed herself to feel the full weight of the
past days—the humiliation of being accused, the cold terror of
the streets, the relief of vindication. But alongside these came a
bitter undercurrent she scarcely recognised in herself.

She had prided herself on her forgiveness, her ability to see
God's hand even in hardship. Yet now, remembering the whispers, the suspicious glances, the immediate assumption of her
guilt simply because of where she came from—Mercy found
forgiveness elusive.

"Is this what I've become?" she whispered to the empty
room. "Someone who holds grudges?"

A soft knock interrupted her thoughts. Simon's voice came
through the door. "Mercy? May I speak with you?"

She hesitated, straightening her apron before opening the
door. Simon stood awkwardly in the narrow corridor, too tall
for the servants' quarters, his presence an anomaly here.

"You shouldn't be up here," she said. "It isn't proper."

"I know." He glanced around, then gestured to the stairs.
"Would you walk with me in the garden instead? It's quiet
there."

The December air was crisp as they followed the gravel

path between dormant rosebushes. Their breath formed clouds in the fading afternoon light.

"How does it feel?" Simon asked. "Being back?"

"Strange," Mercy admitted. "Like wearing a glove that once fit perfectly but has somehow been altered."

"It will take time. For everyone."

"Some may never see me the same way again."

Simon stopped, turning to face her. "Their opinions aren't what matter. Those who truly knew you never doubted your character."

"You didn't," she acknowledged softly. "Even when the evidence seemed against me."

"I know who you are, Mercy Whitfield." His eyes held hers, sincere and unwavering. "You are not defined by where you come from; you are defined by who you are. Your compassion, your faith, your strength—these are what I see when I look at you."

His words warmed something deep within her, yet brought a fresh ache too. "Simon ..."

"I've been thinking," he continued, his voice gathering conviction. "About my future. About the mission work we started together."

"I was afraid they might forbid you to continue it."

"Nobody can forbid me from following my heart." He took her hand, his fingers warm against her cold ones. "Mercy, I believe God brought us together for a purpose. Your understanding of hardship, my position to affect change—together we could do so much good."

Mercy felt her heart quicken at his words, at the implication behind them. Yet alongside hope bloomed fear—fear of reaching beyond her station, of bringing scandal to this man who had shown her nothing but kindness.

"Simon," she said carefully, withdrawing her hand, "I think

perhaps the excitement of proving my innocence has carried you away. You're speaking of things that can't be."

"Why can't they?"

"You know why." She looked away, toward the grand house that represented everything she was not. "I'm a housemaid from Seven Dials. You're the son of Lord Belmont. Some differences cannot be bridged, no matter how we might wish it."

"I don't believe that."

"Then you're being naïve." The words came out sharper than she intended. "Think of what people would say. Think of what your position would become if you aligned yourself with someone like me."

"Someone like you," he repeated slowly. "And what exactly is that, Mercy? Someone honest? Someone faithful? Someone with more courage and wisdom than most people twice your age?"

Despite herself, tears pricked at Mercy's eyes. "Simon, please. Don't make this harder than it already is."

He stepped closer, his presence a shelter against the winter chill. "I'm not trying to make things difficult. I'm trying to show you what I see so clearly—that together, we could build something meaningful."

Mercy looked up at him, this man who had defended her when no one else would, who saw in her what she scarcely dared see in herself. The yearning to believe him, to accept what he offered, was almost overwhelming.

But fear held her back—fear that his feelings stemmed from pity rather than love, fear that he would one day regret choosing someone so far beneath his station, fear that she would bring him nothing but hardship in a world that would never truly accept such a match.

"I need time," she whispered. "This is all happening so fast."

Simon nodded, disappointment visible in his eyes though he tried to hide it. "Of course. Take all the time you need."

As they walked back toward the house in silence, Mercy felt the weight of what remained unspoken between them—his hope, her hesitation, and the uncertain path that lay ahead.

56
MRS MARSH'S ADVICE

The brass clock on the mantle ticked steadily as Mercy folded linens in the small back parlour. She'd returned to her duties two days ago, yet the rhythm of the household felt different now—faces that once smiled warmly now held caution, conversations hushed when she entered rooms. The servants who believed in her innocence welcomed her back with open arms, while others maintained a wary distance.

"Your thoughts are louder than that clock, child."

Mercy started, nearly dropping the sheet in her hands. Mrs Marsh stood in the doorway, her keen grey eyes missing nothing.

"I'm sorry, Mrs Marsh. I was woolgathering."

"It wasn't a criticism." The housekeeper closed the door behind her and approached the table. "May I join you?"

Mercy nodded, and Mrs Marsh took up a pillowcase, her practiced hands making quick work of the folds.

"I saw you walking with Mr Simon in the garden yesterday," Mrs Marsh said, her tone casual but her gaze intent. "And again this afternoon."

Heat rose to Mercy's cheeks. "I know it's not proper, but—"

"I didn't come to scold you." Mrs Marsh set down the folded linen and fixed Mercy with a direct look. "I came because I see the turmoil in your eyes, clear as day."

Mercy's hands stilled. "Is it so obvious?"

"Only to those who know what to look for." Mrs Marsh's voice softened. "You care for him, don't you?"

The question hung in the air between them. Mercy had scarcely admitted it to herself, let alone spoken it aloud.

"It doesn't matter what I feel," she finally said. "Mr Simon deserves someone of his own station."

Mrs Marsh made a sound—half laugh, half snort. "And who decided that? The same people who were quick to believe you a thief because of where you were born?"

"The world we live in—"

"Is full of rules made by people, not by God." Mrs Marsh took Mercy's hands in her own. "Listen to me, girl. I've served in great houses for forty years. I've seen marriages made for advantage that brought nothing but misery, and I've seen love between the most unlikely people create something beautiful."

Mercy blinked back sudden tears. "But the difference between us—"

"Love and character matter more than birth," Mrs Marsh said firmly. "Simon's calling is to serve the poor, isn't it? Who better to help him than someone who truly understands those struggles?"

"But his family—"

"His family condemned an innocent girl without proof," Mrs Marsh reminded her. "Perhaps they've learned something from that mistake."

The words resonated in Mercy's heart, offering a sliver of possibility she'd been afraid to consider.

"Think on it," Mrs Marsh patted her hand before rising.

"And remember—God rarely works through the expected channels."

57
THE HUMAN HEART

Three days later, Mercy sat in the small chapel attached to the Belmont house. Early morning light filtered through stained glass, casting coloured patterns across the stone floor. She'd been turning Mrs Marsh's words over in her mind, searching for clarity.

The chapel door opened, and Mercy turned, expecting Simon. Instead, Father McKinnon entered, his familiar kind face a welcome sight.

"Father!" She rose quickly, surprise giving way to joy. "What are "

"Simon sent for me." He smiled, taking a seat beside her. "He thought you might need a familiar ear."

Warmth spread through Mercy's chest at Simon's thoughtfulness. "He's very kind."

"He's more than kind, I think." Father McKinnon's eyes twinkled. "He's a man who knows his own mind and heart."

Mercy looked down at her hands. "That's what frightens me. What if his heart is leading him toward something that will only bring him hardship?"

"Ah." Father McKinnon nodded slowly. "So that's the trouble."

"Father, the world doesn't allow people like me to marry people like him. It just doesn't."

"The world has many opinions on what should and shouldn't be." He leaned back against the wooden pew. "But I find Scripture often tells a different story. Did you know King David married a shepherd's daughter? Moses married outside his people entirely. Ruth was a foreigner who married into the lineage that would one day produce our Saviour."

Mercy considered this. "Those were different times."

"Were they?" Father McKinnon smiled gently. "Human hearts haven't changed so very much across the centuries. And neither has God's habit of using unlikely partnerships for His purposes."

"But what about the scandal? The whispers? The doors that might close to him?"

"Those are real concerns," he acknowledged. "But consider this—Simon's calling is to serve those society has forgotten. Perhaps having a wife who understands that world firsthand isn't a liability but precisely what he needs."

A flutter of hope stirred in Mercy's chest. "Do you truly believe that?"

"I believe God never makes mistakes in the people He brings together." Father McKinnon's gaze was steady. "The question is not whether others will approve, but whether you are willing to be brave enough to accept what's being offered."

58
YES

The mansion garden bloomed with early spring flowers as Mercy walked alongside Simon that evening. The conversations with Mrs Marsh and Father McKinnon had planted seeds of possibility in her heart, yet doubt still clung stubbornly to her thoughts.

"You've been quiet today," Simon observed, his voice gentle. "Is something troubling you?"

Mercy paused beside a budding rosebush. "I've been thinking about what you said the other day—about us having a purpose together."

Simon's expression brightened. "And?"

"And I'm still afraid," she admitted. "Not of hardship or work—I've known plenty of both. I'm afraid of being the reason you lose standing in society, of doors closing to you because of me."

"Mercy," Simon took her hands in his, "the doors I care about are the ones that lead to doing God's work. Everything else is just ... decoration."

"Your family—"

"My family has seen your character tested in fire and proven true." His thumbs traced circles on her palms. "Father regrets his hasty judgment. Mother has always admired your skill and grace. Even Constance seems chastened by recent events."

"But will they accept me as more than a servant? As your —" She couldn't finish the sentence.

"As my wife?" Simon completed softly. His eyes held hers, steady and certain. "That's what I'm asking, Mercy. Will you marry me? Will you join your life with mine, your gifts with mine, to serve God and those He loves?"

Mercy's heart raced, joy and fear warring within her. "Simon, are you certain? Truly certain?"

"I have never been more certain of anything in my life." He knelt before her on the garden path, still holding her hands. "Mercy Whitfield, I love you. I love your compassion, your wisdom, your strength. Will you be my wife?"

Tears spilled down Mercy's cheeks as she looked at this man—this good, kind man who saw her clearly and loved what he saw. The words of those who cared for her echoed in her mind: Mrs Marsh's wisdom about love and character, Father McKinnon's reminder of God's unexpected partnerships.

Perhaps this unlikely love was not a mistake but a gift. Perhaps together, they could build something more beautiful than either could create alone.

"Yes," she whispered, her voice steadying as conviction grew. "Yes, Simon, I will marry you."

Joy transformed his face as he rose and gathered her in his arms, his embrace warm and secure. As she rested her head against his chest, Mercy felt the last of her doubts begin to dissolve, replaced by the tremulous hope of new beginnings.

59
JUST MERCY

The pale moonlight sliced through the attic window of Mercy's room as she crept along the servants' corridor. She couldn't possibly sleep—not with her heart beating a wild tattoo against her ribs and Simon's proposal still warm on her lips. She needed to share this impossible news with the only two people who might understand what it meant to her.

Mercy knocked softly on Betsy's door, listening for stirring within. The door cracked open, revealing Betsy's sleep-tousled red curls and puzzled expression.

"Mercy? What's happened?" Betsy rubbed her eyes, pulling a shawl around her nightdress.

"Is something wrong?" Tommy's voice drifted from the end of the corridor where he'd appeared from the men's quarters, concern etched across his features.

Mercy beckoned them both toward the small sitting area where servants sometimes gathered on rare free evenings. The room stood empty now, lit only by the dim glow of a single oil lamp turned low for the night.

"I shouldn't wake you, but—" Mercy's voice caught as the

reality of what had happened in the garden washed over her anew.

"You're trembling." Tommy stepped closer, his brow furrowed. "Has someone upset you?"

Mercy shook her head, a smile breaking through despite her effort to contain it. "Simon asked me to marry him."

Silence stretched for one heartbeat, then two.

"The young master?" Betsy's whisper held disbelief. "And you said ...?"

"I said yes."

Betsy's squeal of delight shattered the midnight quiet. Tommy clapped a hand over her mouth, his own eyes wide with astonishment.

"You'll wake the whole house," he hissed, though his grin belied any real admonishment. He turned to Mercy. "He's asked you proper, then? Not just talking about someday or somehow?"

"Properly. On his knee in the garden." Mercy sank into a chair, still scarcely believing it herself. "After all those conversations about his mission work, about what we might accomplish together in Seven Dials ..."

Betsy dropped to her knees beside Mercy's chair, capturing her hands. "I knew it! The way he looked at you when you nursed that sparrow—like you were performing miracles. And when you were accused of theft, he nearly tore the house apart defending you."

"Mrs Belmont will have kittens," Tommy mused, though his eyes danced with mischief. "Proper London society might never recover."

"You're not helping," Betsy scolded, though she couldn't suppress her own giggles.

"We're telling his parents tomorrow morning," Mercy said, her stomach knotting at the thought. Lord Belmont had apologised for his hasty judgment regarding the necklace, but accepting her as a daughter-in-law was an entirely different matter. "Simon believes they'll come around, given time."

"They will," Tommy said with unexpected conviction. "They're fair people, underneath it all. And Simon's made of the same stubborn stuff as his father—he won't be moved once he's made up his mind."

"And anyone with eyes can see you're perfect for each other," Betsy added, squeezing Mercy's hands. "What will you wear? When will you marry? Where will you live?"

Mercy laughed softly. "So many questions I haven't even asked myself yet. All I know is that tomorrow we face his family, and after that ..." She took a deep breath. "After that, we begin to build something new together."

Tommy reached out to touch her shoulder, his face solemn. "From the gutters of Seven Dials to a proper lady—who'd have thought it?"

"Not a lady," Mercy corrected gently. "A minister's wife. And I'm still just Mercy."

"You've never been 'just' anything," Betsy said firmly. "And now the whole world will see what we've always known."

60

ACCEPTANCE

Mercy stood outside the drawing room door, her hands trembling slightly as she smoothed the front of her best dress. Inside, Lord and Lady Belmont awaited her and Simon for what would surely be the most difficult conversation of her life. Simon's warm hand pressed reassuringly against the small of her back.

"They already know what I'm going to say," Simon whispered. "Father may bluster, but his bark is worse than his bite these days."

Mercy nodded, drawing strength from his certainty. "I'm ready."

The drawing room fell silent as they entered. Lord Charles sat in his leather armchair, fingers steepled beneath his chin, while Lady Elizabeth perched on the edge of the sofa, her posture perfect but her eyes unexpectedly kind. Simon guided Mercy forward, his hand never leaving hers.

"Mother, Father," Simon began, his voice steady. "As I mentioned earlier, I've asked Mercy to be my wife, and she has accepted."

Lord Belmont's expression remained unreadable. "And you're quite determined about this, I suppose?"

"Entirely," Simon replied without hesitation.

Lady Elizabeth studied Mercy's face with new interest. "Mercy, dear, would you mind if Simon allowed us a few moments alone? There are some things I'd like to discuss with you."

Mercy felt a flash of panic, but Simon squeezed her hand reassuringly before reluctantly departing. As the door closed behind him, Mercy stood straight-backed, prepared for whatever might come.

"Please, sit beside me," Lady Elizabeth patted the sofa cushion. When Mercy had settled, Lady Elizabeth continued, "I must confess, when Simon first spoke to us of his intentions, I was ... concerned."

"I understand, my lady," Mercy said softly.

"Do you?" Lady Elizabeth tilted her head. "I wonder if you do. My concern wasn't about your background, Mercy. It was about whether someone raised in such hardship could truly understand what it means to partner with a man like Simon— not in terms of status, but in terms of purpose."

Lord Charles cleared his throat. "What my wife means to say is that Simon has chosen a difficult path. We had hoped for an easier life for him."

"With respect, sir," Mercy replied, finding courage she didn't know she possessed, "I believe Simon has chosen the path God set before him. And while it may not be easy, it's right."

Something shifted in Lord Belmont's expression—a grudging respect, perhaps. He'd been prepared to dismiss her, Mercy realised, but not to hear his own values echoed in her words.

"When you were accused," Lady Elizabeth said softly, "you

showed remarkable dignity. No tears, no pleading—just quiet strength. I've seen ladies of the highest birth crumble under far less strain." She took Mercy's hand between her own. "That's when I began to see what Simon sees in you."

Lord Belmont rose and walked to the window, his back to them. "The scandal will be considerable."

"Charles," Lady Elizabeth's voice carried a gentle warning. "We agreed."

He turned, his shoulders dropping slightly. "Yes, yes, we did." He faced Mercy directly. "My son believes that your understanding of poverty and struggle will make you an asset in his work. After recent events, I find myself ... reconsidering my assumptions."

Mercy hardly dared breathe as Lord Belmont continued.

"Simon has always been his own man, even as a boy. Fighting him would be futile, I see that now." A hint of a smile crossed his face. "Perhaps it's time I learned to listen to my son. And to you, Mercy."

"Thank you, sir," Mercy whispered, her voice thick with emotion.

Lady Elizabeth squeezed her hand. "We have much to discuss about the wedding, of course. Nothing too grand—I understand that wouldn't suit either of you. But proper, nonetheless."

The door opened, and Simon returned, tension visible in every line of his body until he saw Mercy's face. His shoulders relaxed as he crossed to her side.

"It appears congratulations are in order," Lord Belmont said gruffly, extending his hand to his son.

THREE DAYS LATER, Mercy was arranging flowers in the morning room when Constance entered, hovering uncertainly at the door.

"May I speak with you, Mercy?"

Mercy nodded, surprised by Constance's uncharacteristic hesitation.

Constance twisted her hands together. "I've been terrible to you, haven't I?"

"Miss Constance—"

"No, please, let me say this." Constance moved closer. "When you first came, I thought nothing of you. Then when you fixed my gown—that beautiful embroidery—I was grateful but also ... envious. You created something I never could, despite all my advantages."

Mercy placed her shears on the table, giving Constance her full attention.

"Then when Simon began spending time with you ..." Constance's voice faltered. "I was jealous and petty. I listened to Margaret's gossip, and worse, I encouraged it. When the necklace went missing, I wanted to believe you'd taken it."

Tears spilled down Constance's cheeks. "I'm so sorry, Mercy. I've learned so much through this experience, and I hope you can forgive me."

Mercy felt a swell of compassion for this young woman who had everything yet struggled with her own insecurities.

"There's nothing to forgive," Mercy said gently. "We were never in competition, you know. Not for anything."

"I know that now." Constance wiped her tears and gave a watery smile. "Simon chose well. Better than I would have chosen for him, I admit."

"Perhaps," Mercy suggested carefully, "we might start anew? Not as mistress and servant, but as ..."

"Sisters?" Constance offered. "I've never had a sister."

"Neither have I," Mercy replied, smiling as Constance spontaneously embraced her.

61
NOTICED

As spring advanced, the Belmont household gradually adjusted to the changing dynamics. At Lady Elizabeth's insistence, Mercy now took tea in the drawing room and dined with the family when no guests were present. Lord Belmont, initially stiff in these situations, gradually unbent enough to ask Mercy's opinion on matters related to the poor in the East End.

"You understand their needs better than any charity committee I've sat on," Lady Elizabeth remarked one evening as they discussed a proposed soup kitchen.

"That's kind of you to say, my lady."

"Elizabeth, please," she corrected gently. "We shall be family soon enough."

Mercy caught Simon's eye across the room, his smile filled with quiet joy. She had worried their relationship would cost him his family's respect, but instead, it seemed to be forging new connections between them all.

Later that night, Mercy walked with Simon in the garden, now filled with blooming daffodils and early roses.

"Are you happy, Mercy?" Simon asked, his arm warm around her waist.

She considered the question, thinking of her journey from the tenements of Seven Dials to this moment. "I never imagined this life," she admitted. "After Mother died, I thought I'd lost everything."

"And now?"

Mercy smiled, watching a robin tend to its nest in a nearby tree. "Now I understand what Mother meant when she said God notices every sparrow that falls. He noticed me too."

Simon pressed a kiss to her forehead. "As did I. And I always will."

As twilight deepened around them, Mercy allowed herself to embrace the future taking shape—a life of purpose, of service to others, and of love that had overcome every barrier placed in its path.

62

PROMISES

Mercy stood in the vestry of St Dunstan's Church, watching her reflection in the modest looking glass Mrs Campbell had provided. Her wedding gown was simple—cream-coloured silk with delicate embroidery she'd worked herself—forget-me-nots woven with silver thread around the neckline and cuffs.

"You look beautiful," Betsy breathed, adjusting the small wreath of fresh flowers crowning Mercy's dark hair. "Like an angel, truly."

"Not like a girl from Seven Dials at all," Mercy replied with a soft laugh.

Mrs Marsh stepped forward, her usually stern face softened with pride. "You look exactly like what you are—a woman who has earned every moment of happiness through your own goodness and strength."

Mercy blinked back tears, not wanting to spoil the kohl Betsy had carefully applied to her eyes. These women—one who'd guided her through service in a grand house, the other who'd shared laughter in steaming kitchens—had become the family she thought lost forever.

"I wish Mother could see this," Mercy whispered.

Mrs Marsh pressed something cool into Mercy's palm. "Your mother sees. And she'd want you to have this today."

Mercy opened her hand to find Mrs Campbell's silver thimble—the one given to her when she'd first left St Dunstan's. "I can't take this back—"

"You're not taking it back. You're carrying it forward," Mrs Marsh said firmly. "Something old to begin something new."

A knock at the vestry door announced Father McKinnon, his kind eyes crinkling at the corners when he saw her. "It's time, Mercy. Are you ready?"

The chapel looked nothing like Mercy remembered from her darkest days. Sunlight streamed through the windows, illuminating the simple altar adorned with spring flowers. Simon waited there, standing tall in his dark suit, Tommy beside him with a grin that threatened to split his face.

As Mercy stepped into the aisle, she felt a profound sense of homecoming. The modest pews held an unlikely gathering— the Belmont family sat in the front row, Constance dabbing at her eyes with a handkerchief Mercy had embroidered as a peace offering. Behind them sat Cook and the household staff who had travelled from Belgrave Square.

But what brought the lump to Mercy's throat was the back of the chapel, where Pip, Mary, and the other children she'd once sheltered with now sat scrubbed clean and dressed in their Sunday best. Mary clutched a small posy matching Mercy's own bouquet.

With each step toward Simon, Mercy felt the threads of her life weaving together—the girl who had huddled in doorways, the seamstress who had created beauty from scraps, the woman who had found her purpose in both grand houses and humble streets.

Simon took her hands in his, his brown eyes never leaving hers as Father McKinnon began the ceremony. The familiar words washed over her—promises of love, honor, faithfulness. When Simon slipped the gold band onto her finger, she thought of all the impossible distances they had crossed to reach this moment.

"I, Simon Belmont, take thee, Mercy Whitfield ..."

His voice never wavered, speaking her name with such reverence that she felt wrapped in certainty.

"I, Mercy Whitfield, take thee, Simon Belmont ..."

Her own voice grew stronger with each word, her fingers steady as she placed the matching ring on his finger. They had chosen simple bands, believing that true value lay not in ornamentation but in the promises they contained.

When Father McKinnon pronounced them husband and wife, the chapel erupted in cheers—Tommy's whoop rising above the dignified applause of the Belmonts, the children's excited chatter mixing with Mrs Marsh's discreet sniffling.

Simon's kiss was gentle yet certain, sealing their union before God and this unlikely assembly that represented every chapter of Mercy's journey.

63
A NEW HOME

TWO YEARS LATER...

Afternoon sunlight streamed through the windows of the modest parsonage adjoining St Paul's Church, warming the worn wooden floor where six young girls sat in a semi-circle. Their faces—some smudged despite best efforts at cleanliness, others bearing the hollow-cheeked look of those who knew hunger too well—were intent on the needles in their small hands.

"Careful now, Emily," Mercy guided, adjusting a nine-year-old's fingers on the needle. "Not too tight or the thread will knot."

The girl's tongue poked between her teeth in concentration as she completed her stitch, then looked up with triumph. "Like this, Mrs Belmont?"

"Perfect." Mercy smiled, remembering her own mother's patient guidance at precisely this age. "You've a natural gift."

The humble room bore touches of care despite its

simplicity—curtains Mercy had embroidered with vines and birds, a patchwork quilt draped over the settee, and shelves of well-worn books alongside threads and fabrics. From these modest surroundings, she and Simon had built something remarkable over the past two years. Simon and Mercy had picked this church in Seven Dials specifically.

"Mrs Belmont, tell us again about Joseph's coat," piped up Lily, the youngest at barely seven, whose stitches remained uneven but whose enthusiasm never wavered.

"Very well," Mercy nodded, reaching for her mother's Bible. Its leather cover had grown softer with the years, its pages marked with pressed flowers and notes. "Joseph's father made him a coat of many colours ..."

As Mercy read, her fingers continued working, guiding the thread through linen with practiced precision. The girls listened, occasionally asking questions that connected the ancient story to their own lives in Seven Dials. They understood what it meant to be forgotten, to struggle, to hope against hope.

"So Joseph forgave his brothers, even after they'd been so cruel?" asked Mary, now twelve and showing remarkable skill with detailed embroidery patterns.

"Yes," Mercy answered. "Sometimes forgiveness is the hardest stitch of all to master, but it creates the most beautiful pattern in the end."

Through the window, Mercy caught sight of Simon in the small church garden. His tall figure bent toward Tommy as they examined something among the vegetables they grew to supplement the soup kitchen. Though Simon wore the collar of his station, his sleeves were rolled up, hands dirty from the work he never considered beneath him.

Tommy had transformed as much as she had. No longer

"Quick-Fingers" of the street, he'd become Thomas Hatch properly, the church's groundskeeper and a leader to the local boys who once might have turned to picking pockets. His gestures were animated as always, making Simon laugh at whatever tale he was telling.

The silver thimble on Mercy's finger caught the afternoon light as she guided her needle. Mrs Campbell's gift had travelled with her through every stage of her journey—from frightened girl to housemaid to minister's wife. The old Scotswoman had passed away peacefully last winter, leaving Mercy with a deeper understanding of how lives could be stitched together across time through small acts of kindness.

"Ladies, mind the time," Mercy reminded gently. "Your mothers will be expecting you home to help with supper."

As the girls gathered their work, carefully placing it in the small cloth bags Mercy had made for each of them, she marvelled at how her childhood dreams had taken form. Not in grandeur or wealth, but in this—creating beauty where there had been none, teaching skills that might lift these children beyond the circumstances of their birth.

"Same time Thursday, Mrs Belmont?" asked Emily, carefully tucking her needle into the small cushion Mercy had taught them to make.

"I'll be here," Mercy promised, helping the smallest girl with her coat buttons. "And perhaps we'll start on handkerchiefs next week."

After the girls departed in a flurry of thank-yous and curtsies, Mercy stood in the doorway watching them navigate the familiar streets of Seven Dials—streets that had once seemed so threatening to her, now transformed by purpose.

The needle rested in her hand, warm and comfortable. From this simple tool, her mother had taught her to create beauty. From that lesson, she had built a life that spanned worlds no one thought she could bridge.

God notices every sparrow that falls, her mother had said. And He had noticed her—not to spare her from falling, but to ensure she had the strength to rise again.

THE FIRST CHAPTER OF 'THE LOST ORPHAN'S FOUND FAMILY'

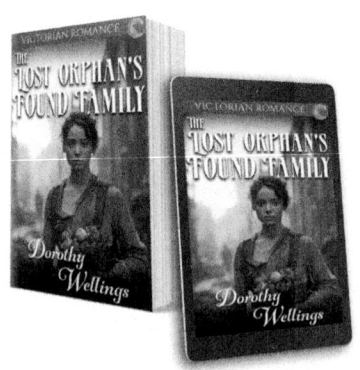

St Catherine's Orphanage stood three stories tall against the pale London sky, its grey stonework mottled with decades of soot and neglect. The morning fog clung to the building like a shroud, softening its hard edges and peeling paint. A wooden sign hung precariously from one rusted chain, the words "St Catherine's Orphanage" barely legible beneath years of weathering.

Inside, the floorboards creaked even when no weight pressed upon them, as if the building itself sighed in its sleep. Corridors stretched in dim procession, lined with doors to dormitories where children slumbered on thin mattresses. The walls, once a cheerful yellow, had faded to the colour of old parchment, adorned only by the occasional religious print in tarnished frames.

Annabelle's eyes fluttered open before the bell. Her thin blanket provided little comfort against the morning chill, but she'd grown accustomed to such discomforts. Sliding from her narrow bed, her bare feet found the cold floor with practiced precision. She tugged her faded nightgown lower over her knees and stretched her small frame, shoulders rolling back with quiet determination.

The dormitory housed a multitude of children between eight and twelve years old, their breathing creating a gentle symphony of slumber. The older children slept on the floor below. Annabelle moved between the beds with the grace of someone far older than her ten years. At little Emma's bed, she tucked a corner of blanket more securely around the girl's shoulder. The child had arrived just last month, still crying herself to sleep most nights.

"There now," Annabelle whispered, smoothing Emma's tangled hair. "Today might bring something wonderful."

She continued her rounds, adjusting Sarah's pillow and retrieving Lily's stuffed rabbit from where it had fallen. These small kindnesses required no acknowledgment – they were simply what one did for family, even a family cobbled together by circumstance rather than blood.

The grey light of dawn strengthened, casting long shadows across the worn floorboards. Annabelle padded to the window, her movements silent from years of practice. The latch resisted briefly before surrendering with a muted click. She pushed the window outward, letting the morning air flow into the stuffy room.

A cool breeze caressed her face, carrying the promise of another day. The orphanage garden spread below her, modest but meticulously tended. Annabelle's chest expanded with pride at the sight of the daffodils she'd planted last autumn, their yellow heads nodding in greeting. Between the vegetable patches and flowering borders, she'd created a haven of beauty amid desolation.

The scent of earth and green things rose to meet her, washing away the stale indoor air. Annabelle closed her eyes, inhaling deeply. In her mind, she was already kneeling in the soft soil, coaxing reluctant seedlings toward the sun. The garden existed as proof that care could create wonders, even in the most unlikely places.

A shaft of sunlight broke through the clouds, illuminating her face. Annabelle's lips curved into a small smile as the warmth touched her skin. The orphanage walls might be crumbling, the meals meagre, and the winters bitter, but moments like this held their own kind of wealth.

From below came the sound of Mrs Whitmore unlocking the kitchen door, the day's routines beginning their familiar march. Annabelle lingered by the window, watching a robin hop along the garden path. Soon the bell would ring, summoning them to morning prayers and porridge, but for now, this pocket of peace belonged to her alone.

ANNABELLE QUEUED with the other girls, wooden bowl clutched in her small hands, waiting for her morning portion. Mrs Porter, the cook, ladled thin porridge with mechanical efficiency, her weathered face impassive. The dining hall echoed with the scrape of spoons against bowls and muted conversations.

"Thank you," Annabelle murmured when her turn came, earning a flicker of warmth in Mrs Porter's tired eyes.

She ate quickly, savouring the hint of honey—a Sunday treat—and watched sunlight strengthen through grimy windows. The moment prayers ended and breakfast duties were complete, Annabelle slipped outside, her heart quickening as she approached her beloved garden.

The modest plot hugged the eastern wall where morning light lingered longest. Here, amid London's grit and soot, Annabelle had coaxed life from reluctant soil. She knelt on the damp earth, unconcerned about staining her faded dress, and pulled a small trowel from her pocket.

"Good morning," she whispered to a row of sprouting carrots, gently loosening soil around their delicate stems. "You've grown since yesterday, haven't you?"

Her fingers worked methodically, distinguishing between valuable seedlings and encroaching weeds. Each unwanted plant she extracted with care, setting them aside for the compost heap rather than simply discarding them.

"Even weeds have purpose," she often told the younger children. "Nothing God creates is truly worthless."

The garden responded to her touch, as if recognizing a kindred spirit. Annabelle hummed softly, a hymn from Sunday service, while pruning back an overeager rosemary bush. The herb's fragrance released into the air, sharp and cleansing.

"What are you doing, Belle?"

Annabelle turned to find five-year-old Clara peering through the wrought iron fence, her small fingers curled around the bars. Behind her stood Phillip and three other young orphans, their curious faces pressed against the metal.

"I'm helping things grow," Annabelle replied, brushing soil from her palms. "Would you like to join me? I've seeds that need planting."

Clara's eyes widened. "Mrs Porter says we mustn't touch the garden."

"Nonsense. How else will you learn?" Annabelle unlatched the gate. "Come, I'll show you."

The children hesitated before Phillip, always the boldest, stepped forward. "What sort of seeds?"

Annabelle reached into her pocket and produced a small paper packet. "Marigolds. They'll bloom bright as sunshine."

This promise of colour in their grey world proved irresistible. Soon all five children knelt beside Annabelle, their small hands eagerly digging shallow trenches under her guidance.

"Gently now," she cautioned when Phillip jabbed too enthusiastically. "Plants are like people—they need tender care to thrive."

Clara placed each tiny seed with solemn concentration. "Will they grow big enough for Mrs Whitmore to see from her window?"

"If we tend them properly." Annabelle demonstrated how to cover the seeds with just the right amount of soil. "Not too deep, or they'll struggle to reach sunlight."

Phillip flicked dirt at another boy, who squealed in protest.

"Phillip," Annabelle said firmly, "gardens need respect as well as care."

His mischievous grin faded. "Sorry, Belle."

They worked together, the children's laughter rippling through the morning air like water over stones. Annabelle showed them how to water the newly planted seeds, using a cracked teapot with measured pours.

"There," she said when they'd finished. "Now they're tucked in safely, ready to dream of becoming flowers."

"How long must we wait?" asked Clara, her voice tinged with the impatience of youth.

"Patience is part of gardening," Annabelle replied, wiping a smudge of dirt from the girl's cheek. "But I promise, the waiting makes the blooming all the sweeter."

**Click here to read the rest of
'The Lost Orphan's Found Family'**

**An inspiring tale of faith, resilience, and love's triumph
over life's greatest challenges.**

TEN-YEAR-OLD ANNABELLE'S world is confined to the stern walls of St Catherine's Orphanage, yet her spirit shines bright as London's gas lamps. Despite the harsh conditions and limited resources, Belle finds joy in tending the orphanage garden, caring for younger children, and reading worn Bible stories by candlelight, her unshakeable faith illuminating even the darkest moments.

When a seemingly respectable couple arrives to adopt Annabelle, she dares to hope her prayers for a loving family have finally been answered. But their true intentions soon force her to make a choice that will change everything.

Cast out into an uncertain world with only her faith to guide her, Annabelle finds work with Jonathan Barton, a traveling merchant whose kind heart matches her own. As they journey together across the English countryside, an unexpected bond begins to form—but can there be any future between an orphan and a gentleman?

Just when Annabelle begins to believe in hope and belonging, shocking revelations about her past threaten to destroy everything she holds dear. Torn between duty and desire, between her origins and her dreams, she must discover what truly makes a family.

Will Annabelle find the courage to fight for love against impossible odds? Can she learn that her greatest inheritance isn't what she was born with, but what she chooses to build?

Follow Annabelle's inspiring journey from orphaned child to beloved wife and mother in this unforgettable story of a young woman who discovers that true family isn't about blood relations, but about the people who choose to love and cherish you.

'The Lost Orphan's Found Family'

OUR GIFT TO YOU

AS A WAY TO SAY THANK YOU WE WOULD LOVE TO SEND YOU THIS BEAUTIFUL STORY FREE OF CHARGE.

Click here for your FREE COPY of

'The Little Orphan Waif's Crusade'

CornerstoneTales.com/sign-up

In the wake of her father's passing, seven-year-old Matilda is determined to heal her sister Effie's shattered spirit.

Desperate to restore joy to Effie's life, Matilda embarks on a daring quest, aided by the gentle-hearted postman, Philip. Together, they weave a plan to ignite the flame of love in Effie's heart once more.

At Cornerstone Tales we publish books you can trust. Great tales without sex or swearing, but with all of the mystery and romance you expect from a great story.

Be the first to know when we release new books, take part in our fun competitions, and get surprise free books in your inbox by signing up to our free VIP Reader list.

As a thank you you'll receive a copy of 'The Little Orphan Waif's Crusade' by *Rachel Downing* straight away, alongside other gifts.

Click here to sign up for our mailing list, and receive your FREE stories.

CornerstoneTales.com/sign-up

LOVE VICTORIAN ROMANCE?

More Dorothy Welling's Victorian Romance

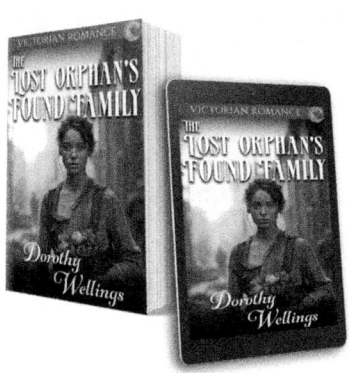

The Lost Orphan's Found Family

Ten-year-old Annabelle's world is confined to the stern walls of St Catherine's Orphanage, yet her spirit shines bright as London's gas lamps. Despite the harsh conditions and limited resources, Belle finds joy in tending the orphanage garden, caring for younger children, and reading worn Bible stories by candlelight, her unshakeable faith illuminating even the darkest moments.

Get 'The Lost Orphan's Found Family' Here!

The Moral Maid's Unjust Trial

Matilda must fend for herself when her father is wrongfully accused for a crime he didn't commit.

Get 'The Moral Maid's Unjust Trial' Here!

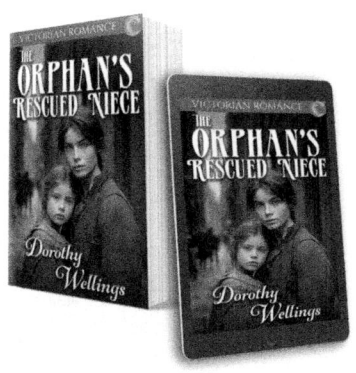

The Orphan's Rescued Niece

As Beatrice grows from a wide-eyed child into a resilient young woman, she finds herself caught between her love for her troubled brother and her desire for a life free from poverty and fear.

Get 'The Orphan's Rescued Niece' Here!

The Bookbinder's Orphan Daughter

Meredith's world crumbles when consumption claims her beloved mother and skilled bookbinder father. When a desperate attempt to find shelter leads her to break into a prestigious house, her life takes an unexpected turn.

Get 'The Bookbinder's Orphan Daughter' Here!

The Lost Orphan of the Parish

Annabelle Sinclair's world shatters when illness claims her beloved parents. Left alone at ten years old with no inheritance, she's sent to the harsh Thornfield Orphanage with nothing but her father's worn Bible and the memories of his gentle teachings.

Get 'The Lost Orphan of the Parish' Here!

The Lost Orphan of the Parish

Grace Hartwell's world is illuminated by her father's love and the warm glow of London's gas lamps he tends each night. Living humbly but happily above a Whitechapel bakery, ten-year-old Grace treasures her father's stories of her saintly mother and learns the healing arts from her mother's cherished prayer book.

Get 'The Orphan Angel's Grace' Here!

Books by our other Victorian Romance Writer *RACHEL DOWNING*

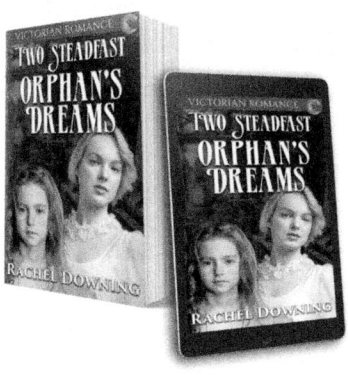

Two Steadfast Orphan's Dreams

Follow the stories of Isabella and Ada as they overcome all odds and find love.

Get 'Two Steadfast Orphan's Dreams' Here!

The Lost Orphans of Dark Streets

Follow the stories of Elizabeth and Molly as they negotiate the dangerous slums and find their place in the world.

Get 'The Lost Orphans of Dark Streets' Here!

The Orphan Prodigy's Stolen Tale

When ten-year-old Isabella Farmerson's world shatters with the tragic loss of her parents, she's thrust into a life of hardship and uncertainty.

Get 'The Orphan Prodigy's Stolen Tale' Here!

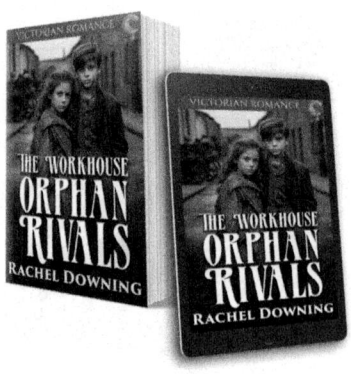

The Workhouse Orphan Rivals

Childhood sweethearts torn apart. A promise broken. A love that refuses to die.

Get 'The Workhouse Orphan Rivals' Here!

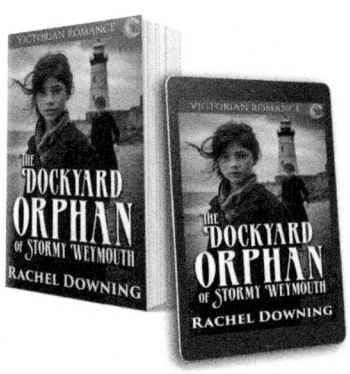

The Dockyard Orphan of Stormy Weymouth

Sarah Campbell's world crumbles when a tragic accident claims her parents' lives. She finds solace in the lighthouse's beam that guides ships to safety. But it's a young fisherman wrestling with his own loss, who truly captures her heart.

Get 'The Dockyard Orphan of Stormy Weymouth' Here!

The Orphan's Christmas Hymn

Seven-year-old Clara Winters' world shatters when tragedy strikes days before Christmas. Sent to St. Mary's Church Orphanage, she finds her only solace in the hymns that once filled her happy home. When her angelic voice catches the attention of the kind-hearted Reverend Thornton and his musically gifted son Edward, Clara dares to dream of a brighter future.

Get 'The Orphan's Christmas Hymn' Here!

The Workhouse Orphan's Redemption

In the brutal world of Victorian London, Emma Redbrook's life begins in tragedy. Orphaned and trapped in Grimshaw's Workhouse, she endures cruelty that would break most spirits. But Emma's unwavering faith becomes her beacon of hope — and her strength.

Get 'The Workhouse Orphan's Redemption' Here!

The Forsaken Lacemaker of Hampstead

Mabel Fairchild's life is shattered by false accusations and devastating loss. With two younger siblings dependent on her care, she makes an impossible promise: to keep her family together despite the world's cruel intentions.

Get 'The Forsaken Lacemaker of Hampstead' Here!

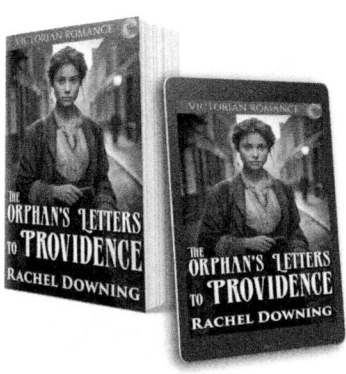

The Orphan's Letters to Providence

In the windswept Yorkshire countryside, Alice Wells's world shatters when tragedy strikes her beloved parents. Orphaned and thrust into a hostile household, she clings to his dying words: "Write to Providence, dear heart."

Get 'The Orphan's Letters to Providence' Here!

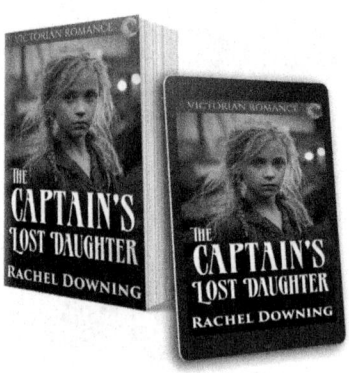

The Captain's Lost Daughter

In 1847, eight-year-old Evangeline's world is torn apart when a violent shipwreck separates her from her beloved father, Captain Thomas Hartwell. Cast adrift and alone, Eva must find the strength to survive in a world that shows no mercy to orphaned children.

Get 'The Captain's Lost Daughter' Here!

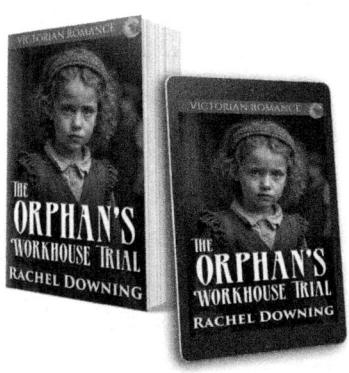

The Orphan's Workhouse Trial

In the harsh industrial landscape of Victorian Manchester, Catherine Whitmore's world crumbles when cholera claims both her beloved parents. Orphaned and alone, she faces an impossible choice that will test the very foundations of her faith.

Get 'The Orphan's Workhouse Trial' Here!

If you enjoyed this story, sign up to our mailing list to be the first to hear about our new releases and any sales and deals we have.

We also want to offer you a Victorian Romance novella - 'The Little Orphan Waif's Crusade' - absolutely free!

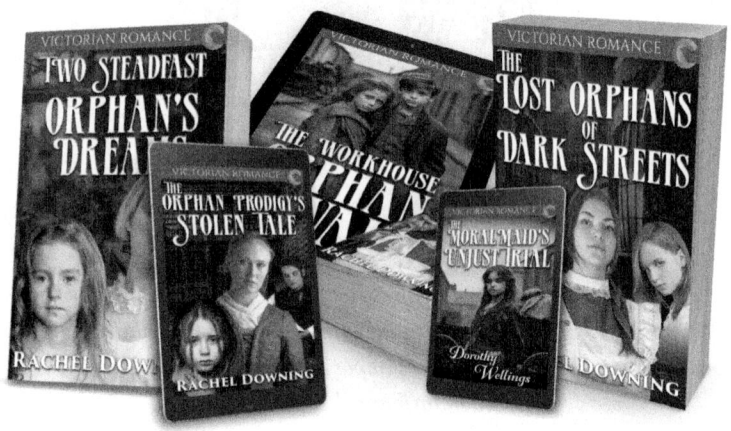

Click here to sign up for our mailing list, and receive your FREE stories.

CornerstoneTales.com/sign-up

Printed in Dunstable, United Kingdom